VIC LEIGH, KRISTIN BOSHEARS, MARIA MARANDOLA, AND TAMMY GODFREY,

Forbidden Love

A Retelling Anthology of Forbidden Loves

First published by Phoenix Voices Publishing 2024

Copyright © 2024 by Vic Leigh, Kristin Boshears, Maria Marandola, and Tammy Godfrey,

All rights reserved. No part of this publication may be reproduced, stored or transmitted in any form or by any means, electronic, mechanical, photocopying, recording, scanning, or otherwise without written permission from the publisher. It is illegal to copy this book, post it to a website, or distribute it by any other means without permission.

This novel is entirely a work of fiction. The names, characters and incidents portrayed in it are the work of the author's imagination. Any resemblance to actual persons, living or dead, events or localities is entirely coincidental.

Vic Leigh, Kristin Boshears, Maria Marandola, and Tammy Godfrey, asserts the moral right to be identified as the author of this work.

Vic Leigh, Kristin Boshears, Maria Marandola, and Tammy Godfrey, has no responsibility for the persistence or accuracy of URLs for external or third-party Internet Websites referred to in this publication and does not guarantee that any content on such Websites is, or will remain, accurate or appropriate.

Designations used by companies to distinguish their products are often claimed as trademarks. All brand names and product names used in this book and on its cover are trade names, service marks, trademarks and registered trademarks of their respective owners. The publishers and the book are not associated with any product or vendor mentioned in this book. None of the companies referenced within the book have endorsed the book.

First edition

*This book was professionally typeset on Reedsy.
Find out more at reedsy.com*

Contents

I   Illicit By Vic Leigh

Chapter One	3
Chapter Two	15
Chapter Three	19

II   Princess Emma Finding A Husband by Tammy Godfrey

Chapter One	25

III   The Island Princess by Kristin Boshears

The Dark Island	47

IV   The Protectors by Maria Marandola

A Warm Welcome Back	65
A Missing Prince	75
The Journey	85
Prince Found	97
Behind the Palace Walls	113
The Tower	122

Wicked Witch 130
Endings & Beginnings 134

Also by Vic Leigh, Kristin Boshears, Maria Marandola, and... 142

Illicit By Vic Leigh

This book is a work of fiction. Names, characters, places, and incidents are the product of the author's imagination or are used fictitiously. Any resemblance to actual events, locations, or persons, living or dead, is coincidental. This book is intended for a mature audience of 18+. There may be some violence, drug use, or other triggers. Please be aware if you have any of those triggers.

Chapter One

Chanelle

"Chanelle, you have six authors wanting to sign with you," my assistant Natalie was stressing.

"I don't have time Nat. I've already got a full plate. My other two copy editors are booked to the hilt, there's no room."

"Make room. One of the authors is J. A. Hinton. Her books are amazing, and she is looking at you to be her editor. With her she brings…"

"Nat, I know. I just don't have time." Damn, Hinton would be good to have. "I tell you what, set up a meeting with each of them, I'll talk with them and see what I can do."

"You're the best Nell," Natalie was over the moon with excitement on the idea of signing some well-known authors.

"I need to run; I'm having my neighbor over for supper tonight."

"What? What about Steve?"

"There is nothing between me and the hot guy next door. In

fact, I'm heading out to see Steve in a few weeks. Make sure that's on my calendar, August 12th."

"It is, but the guy next door. What's going on there?"

"Nothing, he's my neighbor and I'm being neighborly. Now drop it. I've got to finish up the book for Mel, then I'm done for a few days. I need a break. My brain is on overload."

"Okay girl, if you need me, call," Natalie was not happy I didn't give her any details.

"Thanks, I will."

Natalie disconnected and I sighed, what am I doing? What the hell am I doing? I care about Steve, but do I love him? Am I willing to uproot my life and move to the city? But he hasn't proposed, so…oh shit…never mind.

I walk into my small apartment kitchen to get started on dinner. It's not anything special, beef stew and cornbread. It's snowing outside and it sounds good.

My apartment sits in the country with three other small studio apartments. It's one big room basically with a private bathroom. The kitchen has open shelving, a stackable washer/dryer set, a bottom freezer refrigerator, and marble countertops. It's a rustic setting, but I love it. It's small, cozy, and just for me.

After my divorce two years ago, I needed something for just me. I'm far enough away from town that my ex can't just drive by, and I'm close enough that if I need anything I can just run into the store.

My phone goes off and there's a text:

Joe: Are we still on for supper?
Me: Yep, I'm working on it now. Do you work tonight?
Joe: Nope, the roads are too bad, so I'm staying home.
Me: That's good. Supper will be ready in about an hour, come on

Chapter One

over when you want.

Joe: Will do. Thanks.

Joe Mitchell is a damn good-looking muscled, tattooed ex-con. When I moved in, I noticed his damn eyes and smile first. Those eyes could talk you into about anything. They're a golden brown, with a sparkle that I can't explain. And his damn smile could melt the panties off any woman. Damn, I need to be careful with him, but I like his company.

I work on browning the meat and opening several cans of vegetables to add to the stew. My phone dings with a text message again.

Steve: Hey babe, just thinking of you.
Me: Hey sweetheart, damn I miss you.
Steve: I miss you too. I'm going to need to cancel our plans.
Me: What? Why?
Steve: Business
Me: Oh, well okay. I was looking...
Steve: I'll have to get back to you.
Me: Okay, love ya.
Steve: I'll let you know when it's a better time.

I put my phone down and got back to cooking.

Thinking about Steve, he's a great man. He's a good man. I just don't know why he's so busy all of a sudden.

My thoughts are interpreted by someone knocking on the door, must be Joe. No one else is going to knock on my door in this weather.

I put my towel down that I wiped my hands on and move to the front door. Opening it, there he was, all five-ten, a hundred and seventy pounds of gorgeous, muscled man. And that fucking smile, shit.

"Come on in, it's freezing out there." I open the door enough for him to come in.

He hands me a bottle of my favorite Stella Rosa Black wine.

"Thank you, you remembered my favorite."

"Of course, I did. Something smells delicious."

I jump slightly, "Oh shit, it's dinner. I'll be right back. Make yourself comfortable." I head to the kitchen to finish up supper.

He sits down in one of my recliners and says, "What have you done all day?"

"Oh, I'm almost finished editing a book for one of my authors. I started writing some, but that's not going very well, and I had a meeting with my assistant. What have you been doing?"

"Watching TV, fell asleep watching TV, took a shower, that's about it," he laughed.

"Sounds…nonproductive. But you worked last night, right?"

"Yeah, glad I don't have to go in tonight." His voice was almost right behind me, "Need any help?"

I jumped, startled, "Oh, no. It's easy." I nodded to him, "What are you drinking?"

He smiled that damn smile of his, "It's a combination of stuff, not sure what all I put in here." He swirled his cup.

"I see, dinner is almost ready. Can you pour me a glass of wine?" I pulled a wine glass from the shelf and handed it to him.

"Absolutely," he took the glass and opened the wine. He poured a glass and sat it right next to me on the counter. His body was right behind me.

I could feel the heat off his body, it was getting hot in the kitchen, and it wasn't the stove.

His hand moved to my right hip and rested there, "It smells wonderful."

My breath caught and I whispered, "Yeah, it does."

Chapter One

Then I felt his lips on my neck.

I had pulled my hair up into a messy bun, had on my black leggings, and a flannel shirt.

His hand moved from my right hip, up my body to my neck, while his lips slightly grazed the left side of my neck. He kissed up to my ear, and whispered, "Damn you look good tonight."

I cleared my throat, "Thank you."

"Could we have dessert first," he kept kissing my neck, down to my shoulder. He moved the collar of my shirt to expose my skin.

I rolled my neck back, "I didn't fix a…dessert…shit."

"That's not what I'm talking about," he gently turned me, and his mouth was on mine. It was soft, slow, and needy.

My lips burned with desire and returned the kiss. I slid my arms up and around his neck, pulling him closer.

He took the kiss deeper, harder.

I felt desirable and the space between my legs, yeah, I was fucking wet.

He put his hands on my back, pulled me closer, and ran his hands up my back.

I moaned, I fucking moaned. I couldn't help it.

He pulled back from the kiss and put his forehead on mine, "Damn, I've wanted to do that for a year now."

I stood up straight, "What? 1 year?" I removed my arms from his shoulders, and placed my hands on his chest, pushing slightly, "Wait…you have a girlfriend."

He lowered his head, "Yeah."

"Then what is this? What are you doing?"

"I've wanted you for a fucking year."

"Then why didn't you say something before you had a girlfriend? And before I had a boyfriend? Shit…I have a boyfriend."

He stepped back, "Damn, I'm an ass."

"No, you're human and a man, sometimes it's the same thing," I smiled.

He smiled, damn him and that smile. Then he looked at me with those sultry eyes.

"Stop with the puppy dog eyes," I laughed.

"Puppy dog eyes, really," he smiled bigger.

"Damn it," I pulled myself together, "It's time to eat."

He stepped toward me again, "Okay," smiling.

"No…food…that's what I meant." I moved to the stove to finish getting everything ready.

He backed up, "Um…okay. I'll try to behave."

"Good, here…" I handed him a bowl of stew. "There's some cornbread if you want some."

"Thanks for dinner. I really appreciate it."

"It's nothing. You were out here and weren't going to work, I was out here, it's too much food for one person, so…"

"Chenelle, listen. I didn't mean…oh hell…yes, I did. I wanted to kiss you as much as you wanted to kiss me."

"That doesn't make it right Joe. I happen to have a boyfriend."

"Has he asked you to marry him? Is it serious?"

"No, and not yet. But I think he might. Are you asking Jade to marry you?"

"No, she's twenty-five. She's too young for me to marry."

"Oh, come on, how old are you? Thirty?"

"Thirty-five and I'm getting older by the day."

"That's not old…I'm forty-five. Joe, that's ten years between us."

"That's not old. You are gorgeous and don't look forty-five."

"Doesn't change the fact that I am."

Chapter One

He sat his bowl on the counter, "They don't have to know."

I looked at him in shock, "I would know. I can't cheat."

He picked up my glass of wine and handed it to me, "Here, relax. You aren't cheating."

I took a sip, "No, I will not cheat on my boyfriend."

"You're not married. It's not cheating. Where does he live?"

"In the City, I was supposed to be going up there in a few weeks to see him, but he told me he couldn't, so."

"He canceled your plans, why?"

"He said he had to work."

"He's up to something. How often do you see him?"

"Not very often. Usually once a month or so. He's really busy with work."

"What does he do?"

"He works for a ranch up by Terrell County and runs horses, he's busy."

Joe moved to the table that is between the living room and kitchen. He just sat there and started eating his stew and didn't say another word about Steve.

"How's Jade?"

"She's okay. She's fucking young that's for sure."

"What's that supposed to mean? Most men love younger women."

"She's great, but I'm not sure she's for the long haul, ya know. Someday, I want to get married. She's not ready for that. She wants kids, I don't."

"Why don't you want kids?"

"I don't necessarily not want kids, but I don't really want kids this late in life. You have kids, right?"

"Yes, I have two. They are now grown, and one is finishing up her last year in college. Both my girls are going on to careers in education."

"That's great. Kids were never part of my plan. After I got out of prison…"

"Tell me what happened?"

"I was young and stupid. I was seventeen. I was where I wasn't supposed to be, at a party. Everyone was drinking. One of my friends, she was fourteen, this older guy kept messing with her. She told him to stop, but he wouldn't. I had a hothead back then and kinda lost myself. I went after the guy. Beat the shit out of him. He came after me and I pulled a knife. Well, I didn't mean to, but I stabbed him and killed him."

"Oh shit."

"I had a public defender, and the judge gave me life. But I was able to get out on parole after seven years. I was on probation until just a few years ago."

"Oh shit, Joe that's terrible. I'm sorry you had to go through that. You were acting in self-defense, why didn't your attorney use that defense?"

"He wasn't getting paid by me, so he really didn't care," he gave me a sad look.

"Joe, that sucks. I'm sorry. That's terrible," my look must have said it all.

He shrugged, "It's over, so…"

I let it drop. He's paid his dues, and I didn't want to talk about it anymore and I don't think he did either.

"Tell me about your tattoos. I need to get another one, the damn things are addictive." I smiled at him.

"I got several in jail, but this one I got from the tattoo shop on Dearmon and Main. There's a really great guy in there that knows what he's doing," he pulls his shirt off.

Oh…my…God…he's built like a Mac Truck. And his abs,

Chapter One

shit…that damn V going down into his sweats…oh my God!

"This one I got in the city," he's pointing to one that is on his upper chest, left peck.

It's of a raven, its mouth is open with the beak pointed to the sky or up and the wings are spread out and go up under his arm and his back…holy fucking shit…I'm in trouble.

"Um…damn, those are nice." I couldn't finish what I wanted to say, *you're one sexy ass man with some nice ass tattoos.* But I couldn't say that.

He smiled that damn smile and I knew I was going to be a goner. He stood from the chair, sat his empty bowl on the table, and moved in my direction, shirtless.

I just sat there, numb, and not backing away.

He stood in front of me, bent down, and took my hand, pulling me up to him as he stood.

My hands went to his chest, his bare, hard as fuck, chest.

He leaned down and his mouth seduced mine. His lips are soft and so fucking sensual. As his tongue passed over my lips and entered my mouth, I went weak in the knees. His tongue dominated and moved slowly around tasting and feeling every part of mine.

I could feel his hand on the back of my neck, gently messaging my neck as he continued to caress my mouth with his. Damn the man could kiss.

His other hand pulled me into him at my waist, holding me there.

I wasn't moving that's for sure.

His lips moved from my mouth to my neck, kissing his way to my ear. His breath was hot on my ear, "I want you…now."

I moaned and my hands wrapped around his neck giving him the go-ahead.

He moved his hands up and down my back, down to my ass, massaging his way down grabbing my butt and squeezing. His mouth was moving down to my shoulder, that spot just between my neck and shoulder.

I tilted my head to the side giving him better access and fucking moaned again.

This was torcher. He was moving slow, touching, and moving, tasting as he went. His hand that was on my neck was moving slowly down to the front of my flannel shirt.

I felt the buttons being moved and my shirt was then discarded. I didn't have a bra on, and I was now standing there with my boobs out and exposed.

His hand moved to cup one of my breasts. He began to massage and pull at my nipple.

I couldn't help but moan out loud again. I threw my head back allowing him to continue.

His mouth moved to my nipple and his other hand moved to my other breast. He nipped and bit lightly at my nipple causing me to continue moaning into his touch. He moved his mouth to my other nipple and tortured it in the same manner and it felt so wonderful.

In my euphoric state, I allowed him to continue molesting my body, and damn if I didn't like it.

He stood, straight up, looked into my eyes, and smiled that delicious smile of his, "You are gorgeous."

I think the blush on my skin started at my belly button and moved all the way up to my hairline.

He laughed, "You are. Come…" he took my hand and gently pulled me toward my bed. He turned as we made it to the bed, pulled my leggings over my hips, and let them slide down my legs.

Chapter One

I had taken a shower earlier and of course, had no panties on. There I am, standing in front of him, stark naked. What the hell am I doing?

"Damn woman, you've got to know how beautiful you are," he licked his lips and turned me so that the back of my knees hit the mattress. He gently pushed me down and I sat down on the bed. "Lay back, Babe."

I fell back onto the bed with my legs still dangling over the edge, again, what am I doing? "Joe…"

"Shhh…I'm going to take real good care of you. You have been left alone for way too long." He moved his hands up each of my thighs and gently pulled them apart spreading my legs.

"Um…Joe…I…damn…"

He laughed, "It's okay, I know what I'm doing. I'm going to make you feel so good."

"Oh Joe, damn…" I threw my arm over my eyes; how can this be happening? I want it to, but why? Because it feels so good to be wanted, that's why.

I felt his mouth on my right thigh, he was kissing his way toward my pussy. I could feel how wet I was, and I was getting wetter by the second. I could feel his hot breath climbing toward my very sensitive clit.

My heart rate was climbing higher and higher as his mouth got closer to paradise.

Then I felt his mouth, actually, his tongue, flicked my clit a few times before he sucked it into his mouth.

My voice caught in my throat, "Oh shit…"

His tongue began to move faster, his hands were massaging my thighs and pushing them farther apart. His tongue was complete magic, then he sucked my clit into his mouth and bit down.

"Oh…fucking hell…damn…I'm so…close."

I could feel him smile into my wetness. I felt his hands move up, his thumbs were at the base of my pussy and his fingers were moving, massaging my pelvic area. Then I felt one of his thumbs enter my pussy.

"God you are so wet," he went back to sucking and manipulating my clit while continuing to penetrate one of his thumbs in my hot wetness. Then his other thumb entered me, now both thumbs were moving.

I raised my back off the bed, shuttering as my orgasm exploded around his thumbs, "Oh…my…God…"

Chapter Two

Joe

She's absolutely the most beautiful woman I've ever seen. When she finally let go, her release was amazing.

"That was fantastic Chanelle. God, you are beautiful."

I didn't let her come off that orgasm before I was on her again. I pulled my thumbs from her hot wet pussy, licking her essence from both.

She stared at me as I sucked her juices from my thumbs, "Oh shit Joe. That was sexy."

I delved my tongue deep inside her wetness, curling my tongue up into her and moving fast tasting her.

Her hands find my hair, fingers tangled in my short brown hair. This woman was made for me. Is it wrong? Probably. But neither of us have a forever commitment to anyone. She's perfection.

I pull from her pussy, discard my jeans, and my dick is hot, thick, and throbbing. I move over her. Kissing up her breasts, sucking in one nipple then the other.

When I move over her, my dick is so close to that wet pussy, I can feel the moisture on my cock. I look into her beautiful blue eyes. "You ready? I'm going to fuck you long and hard."

All she did was nod.

"I need words, Chanelle. Can I fuck you?" I watch her eyes. She's so close to saying no.

"Yes."

That's all I needed. I plunge my dick deep inside her, hard and fast with no warning.

She gasps, "Fuck…Joe…damn…"

I start moving slow at first and increase my speed as her hips come up to meet each of my thrusts. "Your pussy feels so good wrapped around my cock." I kiss her, tease her lips and tongue.

Her tongue licks and bites at mine.

I pulled back slightly, pounding inside her sweet goodness. "You like that, don't you."

"Yes!"

"You ready to come again?"

"Yes! Please…Joe…"

I lift slightly, raising her legs over my shoulders, she's nearly folded in half. I pound harder and faster than I ever thought I could.

"Yes…fuck…yes…Joe…fuck…fuck…fuck," her orgasm is explosive. Her juices are seeping down my balls.

I slowed down and allowed her to come down from that high. Then I began to move inside her again. I moved myself up on my knees, moving my hips so that my dick thrusts inside her wetness, slow and steady. "Don't take your eyes off mine, Chenelle. Watch my eyes and enjoy it."

Her eyes focus on mine. Her hips moved up to meet each thrust in and out. Slow and steady, this woman is amazing.

Chapter Two

"Joe…I need you to move faster," her eyes stay on mine.

My thumb moved to her clit, I began to rub, soft circles, pinpointing that special place that drives a woman crazy. As my thumb moved and circled the hard little nub, I began to move my hips faster. My dick moving in and out of that wet pussy.

Her hands go to my chest, her hips moved up to meet my movements. "That's a good girl, come again. This time, I'm coming with you. Keep your eyes on me. Good girl."

Her eyes are super focused on mine. Her body responds to every movement I make.

She licks her lips, "I'm coming Joe…come with me."

I moved faster and pushed inside her, she moaned.

Her fingers grasp for my chest, her nails dug in, as her orgasm let go just as my own did.

We both scream each other's names as our essence fills the room. The mixture of mine and hers, the smell is euphoric. I want her more now than I did before.

I thought after I had her, I would be done. Usually, I don't date any one woman. But this woman has hypnotized me, and I need more.

Where the fuck did that come from? I don't need anyone. I proved that repeatedly throughout my time in jail. I need no one and no one deserves me.

I have too much baggage. Too many years in the pen. Too much of me is not good.

"Joe, what are you thinking about?" She is rubbing her hands up and down my chest.

I fall on her, resting my elbows on each side of her head. I look into those baby blue eyes of hers, all I can say is, "You."

She looked puzzled. "Me? What about me?" she is still trying to catch her breath a little bit.

"You are amazing. I don't want this night to end. It's been… incredible." I kiss the tip of her nose.

She takes a deep breath and lets it out, "Joe, there is no commitment here. I see a look in your eyes that you are ready to run."

I laugh, "No, I was just thinking the opposite. I want to curl up next to you and hold you until we can do this again."

Her eyes widen, "Really? It was fantastic. But I didn't think you wanted more than what this was, a one-night stand."

I give her a big smile, "This was no one-night stand, lady. This was…remarkable. And I want to do it again, over and over again."

"Joe…we both have…"

I put my finger to her lips, shushing her. "Let's not go there. We don't need to worry about that. Let's just enjoy this." I roll to the side and pull her with me. I kiss the top of her head. "I need more of you. One night will just not do."

With that, she gave a long sigh. We laid there for awhile without saying a word. After a little bit, I heard her breathing even out and she was asleep. I pulled her closer to me, reached down and pulled the blankets over us. Sleep sounded pretty good to me too.

Chapter Three

Joe

We have seen each other every day for the past two months. I haven't talked to Jade since I slept with Chanelle. She's texted a few times, but I just say I'm busy. She's young, she will move on.

Chanelle broke up with Steve. She found out he was cheating on her.

I pulled into the parking lot of our apartment building. Chanelle is sitting outside in the cold, wrapped in a blanket.

I look at her as I get out of the truck, "What the hell are you doing out here in the cold?"

"It's nice. The sun is shining, and the air is crisp I love it! How was your night at work?" She smiled as she pulled a coffee cup up to her lips.

I can't help but want to be with this woman every day. She amazes me on every level. She's bad ass at work and she's badass in bed. Who could ask for anymore? Not me.

I squat down, so that I can look into her gorgeous blue eyes.

"It was fine. I have something I need to tell you."

She laughed, "Okay. What is it?"

"I know this might seem fast to you, but we have known each other for over a year. I've watched you for over a year."

She laughed again, "Stalker."

I smile, "Not quite. But I need to tell you, in all the women that I've dated, you are the one that I want. You are amazing. I'm in love with you."

Her smile faded and she gasped.

Shit, I just fucked up.

"What? I'm sorry, but I had…"

Her hands cup my cheeks, she pulled me forward, and kissed me. Her warm lips on mine is the best feeling in the world. When she pulled back, she smiled again. "I love you too, Joe."

I laughed softly, "Good, now let's go in. It's freezing. I'll let you warm me up."

"Oh, and just how do you want me to warm me up?"

I pulled her from her sitting position, wrapped her in my arms, and kissed her hard. When I pulled back, I looked deep into her eyes. "We'll see what comes up and you can figure out the rest."

She laughed so hard and so loud; I thought the neighbors down the road might hear. "I'll be more than happy to do whatever, *comes up.*"

"Good, because it's coming up and getting harder."

She pulled me inside the apartment, I shut the door with my foot, and we left the world outside.

It's just her and me, no one else in this world matters.

About the Author

Chapter Three

Vic Leigh is an American Author and has worked in many fields throughout her life. She enjoys reading all authors, but romantic fiction and contemporary romance are her favorites. She is a mother, grandmother, editor, and teacher as well as author. Her small-town romance books are hot, spicy, and addictive.

Keep up to date on new arrivals at all social media sites:
www.vicleighbooks.com
www.facebook.com/vicleighbooks
www.tiktok.com/@vicleighbooks
www.instagram.com/vicleighbooks

II

Princess Emma Finding A Husband by Tammy Godfrey

Chapter One

Princess Emma's parents believed she was prepared to marry and start a family prior to becoming Queen. Despite the challenges, she had children as Queen because her father wanted to meet his grandkids before passing. Despite knowing he lived another twenty years, he always claimed things happened differently.

Several princes have approached her with an offer to make them king if they marry and she becomes Queen. She didn't want this to happen. According to Duke Felix of Kennington, men are the rightful rulers. She will be the ruler of her kingdom, not the wife of a ruler. Princess Emma needed a prince's assistance, not for the purpose of taking over, but to rule as a couple, although they all believed they would take over. When they marry, Duke Felix plans to obtain a degree that would make him King after her father's passing. She only wanted to send him home never to return. His father is just as bad. Instead of recognizing her training to be a ruler, they view her as a babymaker. Out of all the princes and dukes she has spoken to, only two agreed to rule with her, but her staff has different information.

Exhausted from everything, Princess Emma had enough. She was stuck moving from table to table, forced to converse with dull, stuffy men who only wanted her attention because she was a wealthy princess in a stunning dress. Men were attempting to catch her attention by showcasing their bodies, brains, and strength through their attire and gaze. It was normal for her to be surrounded by wealthy, sophisticated individuals every day. Despite enjoying the man's lavish lifestyle, she longed for a day of anonymity, where she would be valued for herself, not her royal status. None of these men desired her for who she truly was. She was desired purely for her status as a wealthy princess.

It was a dark night, evident from the view of the large bay window. She brushed her fingers through her blonde hair, then tucked it away under a hat. Before leaving a group of prestigious individuals, Emma took a deep breath. Pretending to use the bathroom, she actually ran away. She sprinted until she reached the outdoors. She dashed out the side of the palace gate where the maids and footmen emerged. After making it three blocks down, she finally felt relieved and could breathe while walking down Victoria Street, named after her grandmother, the Queen. She reached down and collected mud from the street and applied it to her face in hopes that it would mask her appearance.

As Emma passed by, people on the streets glanced at her, doubting her identity as the princess. She moved swiftly, and eventually she stood alone, away from everyone else. It dawned on her where she was. She observed homeless individuals as she glanced around. Some of them smoke, others hold "will

Chapter One

work for food" signs and some sleep on the concrete.

Emma recocked how her mother used to take her and her brother to visit the less fortunate, teaching them gratitude and exposing them to different walks of life. She intensely gazed at the impoverished individuals who completely disregarded her. Being ignored, strangely enough, brought a sense of contentment. She found a sense of belonging here and could freely express herself.

Emma suddenly experienced a forceful push. She turned to see a man; he didn't look homeless, but rather just mean. With his great height and powerful build, he made quite an impression. Emma was met with the menacing gaze of a man wielding a switch knife and dark brown eyes.

"Give me all your money right now!" the man demanded.

Emma scanned the area, seeking assistance from anyone. Apart from a frail old man, no one was in sight, and he was fast asleep. "Please, I do not want any trouble. Take my small wallet and go away," Emma nervously said, reaching for it only to realize she didn't have it.

The man's searching eyes were fixated on Emma's hands. "Where is the money? You're the Princess. You better have money, or I'll slice your throat!" the man yelled.

"I'm not allowed to carry money around," Emma stated.

Emma felt her heart racing. Is this the way I will die? She thought to herself.

"I'm sorry I don't have money, but you can take her bracelet. It's very expensive," Emma said, struggling to take it off.

The man's patience ran out. Just as he was about to cause harm to Princess Emma, the thrust of the man's knife was suddenly halted, and in the of an eye, he found himself slammed to the ground. Emma shut her eyes, only to discover she was unhurt. As she opened her eyes, she saw a man standing before her, clutching a large cut branch. He was around five feet eleven, a tall individual, with long, dark brown hair and soft brown eyes that somehow gave him a very strong presence. He held the stick in his hands.

"A-are you okay?" he asked her.

Emma nodded. She couldn't take her eyes off this handsome man. He wore baggy blue trousers and an old dark green shirt with leather boots. Was he homeless? He must have been.

"Y-yes, I'm f-fine," Emma stammered.

The young man slowly put the wooden weapon down and looked at the man who lay on the the ground at his feet. The young man completely knocked him out.

"Thank you. You saved my life!" Emma said softly, moving closer to the man.

He smiled, not just any normal smile, but a smile that could make a woman's heart melt. "You're welcome. What are you doing on this side of town, anyway? Shouldn't you be at your castle drinking expensive wine or something?"

Emma laughed. "I guess, but I'd rather not. I was at a party earlier, but I had to get away. Thank you for saving me."

"It's not a big deal. I've had to save a life from time to time. It was the right thing to do."

"Yes, but I want to thank you for helping me," Emma said.

"I don't need your money if that's what you mean," he retorted.

Narrowing her eyes, Emma looked intently. "Are you sure? You are homeless, right?"

The man nodded. "Yes, so? If you believe I helped you solely for personal gain, you're mistaken. I saved you because you are a human being. I would have done the same for anyone."

Chapter One

The man resumed walking away, and Emma couldn't resist trailing after him. "I'm sorry. I didn't mean to be so blunt in asking if you were homeless. I apologize."

Bringing his walk to a halt, the man pivoted to face her. "I'm not ashamed of being homeless. Yes, I don't have my own house, my own bed or nice clothes, but I am happy. I'm pleased."

Smiling, Emma reached out and touched his face. "What's your name?" she asked.

"Why do you want my name? What happens if I choose not to provide my name?"

Emma laughed softly. "You don't have to. I'm sorry, but I feel the need to repay you somehow."

"I already told you that there is no need. Now I have to get going."

He walked off, leaving her behind. Emma waited but then began to follow him once again. "Can I stay a few minutes with you? I don't want to return to the party."

The man nodded. "You're quite the determined princess, aren't you?"

Emma chuckled. "I don't think so."

"Come on now. Come with me and I'll show you where I live."

Emma followed the young man. His long brown hair billowed in the wind as he walked quickly. Emma walked behind him until he finally came to a stop at a park near an oak tree. There was a large makeshift box with a few blankets and a small knapsack. He set his stick down, which he probably used to protect himself. "Well, here is my little home, for tonight that is."

Emma gulped. "You mean you live here?"

The young man laughed. "Well, for tonight I do. The

homeless shelters were full tonight, so I'm stuck out here."

Emma was speechless.

"You can go if you want. I know it's not a proper setting for a proper princess."

"No, I will not go," she responded. "I wanted to spend some time with you, and that's… what I want."

The young man blushed. He turned and took a blanket, spreading it on the grass. "There, you may have a seat."

Slowly, Emma settled herself on the blanket and raised her eyes to meet the young man's. Slowly, he made his way down and smiled at the Princess. "Not exactly a castle, is it?" he asked.

"No, it's not. Can I inquire about what led to your homelessness?"

"I lost my parents a long time ago. My grandmother cared for me, but when my parents passed away, I was left alone. At first, I resided in her home, but I couldn't sustain the expenses, so I switched to a small room at a local Inn. After losing my job, I searched for another, then another, but couldn't find one that paid the bills. I became homeless. I work at a bakery in the village, but the pay is minimal. I'm finding it tough to save money needed for a place call my own.."

"Yes, I can understand," Emma said slowly.

"So I'm here for now."

Emma reached out and put her hand over his. "You are very brave. I admire that about you."

"Thank you."

"It's a beautiful night don't you think?" Emma asked the young man.

He sighed and looked up at the sky. "Yes, it is. I think I will enjoy sleeping out here tonight."

Emma stared at his face. "I don't want you to stay out here.

Chapter One

Why don't you come back to my place, and you can sleep there?"

The young man shook his head. "No, I couldn't do that. Besides, what will your family say if you bring home a homeless young man?"

"Their words hold no importance to me. Please?"

The young man laughed. "Don't worry, sweet Princess, I won't be arrested or anything. I'm happy out here. You are here with me, so why not let us just enjoy this moment?"

Emma chuckled. "You win. I will stay out here with you tonight. I'll try to sleep."

"Lie down on my lap," the young man ordered.

Initially hesitant, Emma couldn't resist in the end. She rested her head on his lap and looked up at him. With a smile on his face, he gently ran his fingers through her hair. His touch was incredible. With just a single touch, she instantly felt calm and comfortable. A beautiful tune escaped his lips as he began to hum, captivating Emma's gaze. The night was adorned with millions of silver stars and a refreshing cool breeze. It seemed like tonight had been untouched by any bad experiences.

"Your hair is so soft. I like running my fingers through it," he whispered.

"I enjoy the sensation of your hand."

The young man kept humming and then started laughing. Emma had a puzzled look on his face. She looked up at him. "What's so funny?"

"Oh nothing. I was reminiscing about when I was a child, and my mother would read me fairytales about a girl who kissed a frog and turned him into a Prince. I can't picture you as a frog."

Emma laughed. "I hope not!"

He looked into her eyes. The moonlight outlined Emma's pretty face. "I can't believe I have you here with me, like this.

It's almost like a dream come true."

"All I need is your name please?" Emma asked.

"Why do you need to know?" he asked.

Emma slowly sat up and touched his face, "I'm here and this is real." She grabbed his hand and put it on her cheek and said, "Close your eyes." His touch was so mesmerizing she felt almost hypnotized. He opened his eyes once again not wanting to miss another look.

"Please tell me your name?" Emma asked.

"Why is it that you insist upon knowing? He smirked "Do you wish to marry your name to mine, to hear how it sounds?"

"That's silly," the princess said, trying not to grin," Don't be so presumptuous. I was merely curious. Calling you by your proper name seems eminently more practical than referring to you as 'my hero' all day and night."

"All day and night?" he asked. "Now is being presumptuous?"

"What do you mean?"

"For how long do you presume to be in my company?"

"Well, I mean…" the blush on her cheeks was becoming more prominent. She turned to look the other way, but only for a moment. When his eyes returned to his, she knew there eas no use in avoiding her feelings, the feelings that overwhelmed her the first moment she laid eyes on him. "I presume to be in your company…your care…your arms, for as long as I can. For as long as you will have me."

"I will have you for all the days and nights to come, but only if you marry me," he said. "I don't want to be King. I want to help you."

"If you marry me you have to promise not to cheat ever, never try to take over when I'm Queen, and to help me help our people in the country," Emma said.

Chapter One

They rose and walked to the church. As they entered, they saw people lying on the pews with blankets trying to sleep. Emma took her hat off and then ran up to her Priest. "Princess Emma, what are you doing here? Where are your guards? Do you need me to get you someone?" The Priest wouldn't stop asking questions.

"I want to get married tonight," she interrupted him.

"To whom, my Princess?" the Priest asked with a questioning look on his face. He looked like he was in his sixties, and the once-brown hair was more gray hair than brown.

"To him," Princess Emma stated.

"You want to marry Duke William of Kennington," the Priest asked.

"You're a Duke?" she gasped, "Why are you on the streets?"

"Not all Dukes have money. When my grandmother died all her money went to my uncle and he didn't want to help me. So, I was left on my own," William said.

"Can we get married now, or do I have to command it?" Princess Emma asked.

"Don't you want your family here?" the Priest asked cautiously.

"No, I want to be married now to William. He's a Duke so no one can complain about it. So, I will marry him now," she stated.

"Yes, my Princess. Do you want the church cleared out for the wedding?"

"No, they can all stay," Princess Emma said. "Can we start now?"

"Yes, we can," the Priest said. Just then they heard the church doors open and her parents came rushing down with guards.

"Honey, where have you been?" the King asked.

"Finding my Prince Charming?" Emma announced.

"Is this who you really want to marry?" the King asked.

"Yes, it is."

"Is that you William? I thought you were in Scotland," the King said.

"No, I have been here the whole time," William stated.

"Were you at the party tonight?" the Queen asked. "Why are you dressed like a commoner?"

"I wasn't at the party tonight," William started, but the King interrupted.

"Is William aware that you will be Queen and he will forever remain a prince?"

William acknowledged his understanding of his duties. "Princess Emma and I discussed it. There's one more thing I'd like to know," he said.

"And that would be…?" the Queen asked with trepidation.

"My uncle and his family abandoned me on the streets after my grandmother's death. Will I have control over my grandmother's money once I become a prince and get married? I mean, will I be the head of the family when I become a prince?"

"I'm confused," the King mentioned, "I heard you were in Scotland studying."

"I inherited a house from my uncle, who deliberately left me with no money for school. I sold the house, got a job, and ended up living on the streets," William recounted.

"You are a beneficiary in your grandmother's will. She leaves almost everything to you when you turn twenty-one," the King told him.

"My uncle said she left me nothing."

"They will fix this after you marry me," Princess Emma reassured him.

Chapter One

"Darling, you're destined to be the next Queen. You must marry in the proper manner." the Queen insisted.

"Emma can do what we did, and how we got married," the King thought aloud.

We will have to do this in my office where people cannot see," the Priest said. "Are we ready, then?"

"Yes, if the Duke and Princess are?" the King said.

It was not the formal occasion that Emma imagined in her youth. No gilded gown or shimmering crown. No trumpets blaring to announce the blessed union. No, this was small, intimate, and perfect.

However, following the completion of the wedding, the queen announced plans to organize a public wedding. While the guards accompanied the Duke and the Princess to his shack to retrieve his bag, they were later escorted back to the castle. "Why did you bring that stick?" William asked his new bride.

"You rescued me using it. Maybe I will need it to save you," Emma said. Upon arrival at the castle, the queen arranged a private room for food and drinks. William, Emma, and her parents gathered to address the issues within William's family.

"Emma, please accompany me," her mother said. Emma found it surprising that she didn't demand. The princess stood up and followed her upstairs to a room beside her own. "I'm aware that you have questions about tonight. It is necessary for someone to observe your consummation on your wedding night," her mom began. "Your father and I got married a month earlier than you are now, and we consummated the marriage privately before having to do it in front of the priest on your wedding day at the church. I think at all the wedding traditions, this was the hardest. Talk to Willam about doing it fast and getting it over with so you can get the males out of your bedchamber. It's very helpful."

"What do I do?" I asked.

"You have complete freedom to do as you please and touch him in any manner you desire. Tonight holds significance for both you and William. There may be discomfort at first, but deep breaths will lessen the pain. Recock the talk we had when the King thought it was time for you to marry?"

"I recock, but still not sure how to take control of the first night together after we get married?" Emma said sheepishly.

"Tomorrow you will be the woman. You and William will talk about it. Recock I talked to you about different ways?"

"I do," Emma said. The talks with her mom have taught her why being together close is important to a marriage.

"Do you want to be in his bed or yours? I'm arranging his bed and bringing in items for tonight. Tomorrow, we'll take care of the rest and have new clothes made for him.

"Yes, mom," Emma said. "I want us to spend tonight in my bed chambers."

"As you wish," Queen said. "Let's get you back to your husband and your father."

As they walked down the stairs, they overheard, "Emma is not marrying you. She marries the son of Duke Felix of Kennington, and he will be King." The voice said. The Queen and princess rushed down the stairs faster, and the guards came running. Emma observed an individual wielding a sword stepping to her husband. She noticed the stick, quickly grabbed it, and before anyone could react, snuck behind the man holding the sword and delivered a powerful blow to the back of his head. Then Emma swiftly swung the stick at the man beside him, incapacitating both.

"Emma, I can't believe you did that," the King said.

Chapter One

"I can. Are we even now?" William asked.

"I think so," Emma said.

"I think the King owes you now," Williams said. "They work for my uncle, Duke Felix of Kennington. My uncle must know I'm here."

"Maxwell," the King said.

"Yes, my King," Maxwell said. He has been the head of the King's guards as long as anyone could recock. He is currently a father teaching his son, who has ambitions of heading the guards.

"Take into custody all cocks of the Kennington family except for William here. When they are in the tower, let me know. You can start the integration tomorrow. I want those two in the tower but with enough distance to prevent communication.

Maxwell confirmed, "Yes, my King," while the guards removed the motionless men from the scene.

"Now it's bedtime for all of us," declared the Queen.

"I completely agree," stated the King.

Each of the rooms received wine and fruit, as mentioned by the Queen. For as long as Emma could recall, the princess's mom and dad have always slept together. Despite being used for childbirth and changing clothes, her mom's room is not where she sleeps with Dad. Despite already having five children, her father mustered the courage to not marry another woman who could only bear one child. According to her father, she fulfilled her duty and will remain with him until the very end.

Her parents have instilled within her the belief that true love is precious, and no one, not even the kingdom, should be able to separate you from the one you love.

William and Emma started up the staircase, telling her parents goodnight, and turned down the hall. She opened the door to his room first. "This is your room, you can set it up any way you want," Emma started. "For tonight I would like you to sleep with me. My parents sleep together every night, I don't know if you want that too?"

"I want to sleep with you every night, even when you're with child I want to be with you," William responded.

With a shaky hand, William stared intensely at her. Emma released his hand, but he continued to touch her face. She slowly moved her hand down to his neck and then his chest. He remained motionless. He continued to let her touch him. Her hand slowly moved downward until it reached his crotch. He gasped, enchanted by the delightful touch of her hand on his cock.

"I've never been with… a man," Emma said softly.

He was taken aback, most princesses wait for marriage, but she was going to be Queen of her kingdom. The fact that this gorgeous girl had never been with a man was hard for him to believe. He put his hand over hers as his cock began to harden. Emma looked down between his legs and then back into his eyes. She smiled shyly.

"I've never been with a woman that way. My Grandmother told me to wait until my wedding night," William said in a whisper.

"You feel hard now," Emma softly said.

"I am hard. I can't begin to explain the level of excitement you've brought me," William told her.

"May I have a look?"

He didn't hesitate and acted immediately. William stepped back, adjusted his belt, and unfastened his pants. Emma relaxed, marveling at the sight. Her eyes were wide with curiosity and anticipation at seeing a man's erection. He took a seat and

Chapter One

exposed his erect cock. There was a sense of numbness about Emma's appearance. She was unable to look away from it.

He took her hand and placed it on his groin. "Touch it."

Her hand glided over his throbbing cock; her eyes fixed on it as if she had never seen anything like it before. "I can feel it throbbing in my hand," she said quietly.

"That's because I'm so excited."

"What does it taste like?" Emma asked boldly.

William felt his heart racing. "Do you want to taste it?"

When she nodded, William put his hands on the sides of her face gently and moved her face downwards to his cock. "Just put it in your mouth slowly and wrap your lips around it."

He immediately felt the warmth of her mouth taking in every inch of his cock. He could feel his toes curling from the intense pleasure. "Ahhh yes, like that! I thought you said you hadn't been with a man?" William asked.

"I haven't. My mom told me what to do to make my husband happy, and not to go to another bed because if I find out my husband is with another, I will kill him," Emma said before returning her attention to what she was going to do with William.

Her lips glided up and down his lengthy shaft with a deliberate and forceful motion. He could sense her tongue swirling, licking, and tasting every part of him. William took a deep breath, closed his eyes, and savored the joy of his happiness. When William felt her stop sucking on his cock, he opened his eyes again. He looked down, and Emma was pulling out his balls.

"Are these the ones responsible for sperm production?" She asked shyly.

William nodded.

"Is it possible to lick and suck on them as well?"

"Y-yes," William said breathlessly.

Her mouth caressed his cum-filled balls, licking them slowly. William watched her slide her pink tongue on his balls and then take turns sucking on them. She could feel his cum boiling, ready to burst out.

"Heaven on earth!" William gasped.

William expressed pleasure as she licked his testicles and stroked his penis with her hand. Emma desired to plead for him to return his penis to her mouth, but the sensation of her mouth on his testicles was unbelievably amazing.

Shortly after, Emma resumed oral stimulation and sensed his impending climax. Her hands cupped his balls and gently squeezed on them as if she was mixing his cum around. She knew it was time to cum. As he tossed his head back, she could feel the first shot of hot cum spurt out with great intensity. Despite feeling him shudder, she persisted in using her mouth on his cock. More cum shot out of his cock and into the Emma's mouth. William was breathless and noticed he was looking down at her. He could tell that she was swallowing his sperm.

She took his cock out of her mouth and quickly swallowed. A smile appeared on her face, and she blushed. "Hmmm, has a distinct taste. I like it."

William was so turned on. He came closer to her and enveloped her in his arms, kissing her with intensity. Their lips moved away from each other, and their tongues met in a sensual dance. He delicately moved her body against his, resulting in her gradually lying back down. Wiliam positioned himself on top and began kissing her neck and face. Emma quietly sighed and moaned. As he sucked on her neck, she could feel his warm breath by her ear.

Chapter One

William moved his hands downward and began raising her shirt. Her flat stomach caught his eye, and before long, her lovely breasts were uncovered. Their size was medium, and their nipples were big and dark brown. He lowered himself and slowly licked the nipple. He felt her arch her back and moan loudly.

"Oooh!"

William then put her nipple in his mouth. He sucked it, holding it in his mouth and then flicking it with his tongue. Taking turns on each nipple, he slid his hands down, touching her belly. He took her nipple out of his mouth and looked at her. She had her eyes closed and her lips were parted as Emma tried to breathe.

Without a word, William trailed his hand and started unfastening her dress. His hand moved downward to remove her shoes. He reached for the ribbons, feeling the soft fabric and parts of Emma's skin. Her hips lifted, hinting at the need to remove her pants. Emma adjusted her dress to cover her knees and then proceeded to remove her shoes. Afterward, she was able to remove her dress completely. She was left lying with but a kirtle on.

Emma grabbed the sides of her kirtle and took it off slowly. William saw Emma's hair from her center. She had a small patch of dark hair, and her lips were small and shut tight, not giving him access to see her.

He used his fingers to open her lips, allowing her clit to become visible. He rubbed it with his index finger and watched her begin to squirm. She bit her bottom lip with a tight grip between her teeth. William slowly dipped a finger inside of her and she yelped so sweetly.

"Hmmmgghhh."

She was so tight, warm and getting more wet each time he slid his finger in and out of her.

"You feel very tight," William rasped.

"I am. I can feel you unraveling my layers. It feels so good."

William removed his finger and licked it. She tasted so incredible. Her soft feminine scent enticed him, and her taste was so delicious. William spread her legs more and knelt between them. He ran his hands up and down her beautiful body, enjoying the feel of her soft skin. Emma moaned and stared up at her.

"You want me to be inside of you?" William asked politely.

"Oh yes. Yes. Please," Emma begged.

William climbed on her and firmly grasped his still erect and pulsating cock. He directed it towards her intimate opening and experienced the sensation of his body being enveloped by her warm inner walls. With a hard gasp, she let out a squeal. "Ouch!"

"I don't want to hurt you." With concern, William stopped moving, and touched her pretty face. "Do you want me to stop?"

"Give me a moment," Emma said, taking deep breaths. "Keep going."

William continued to slide his cock inside of her until she was completely buried in her treasure. He closed his eyes for a few seconds, enjoying her warmth. Gradually, William started to make movements inside her. Initially, it was difficult due to her tightness, but her natural lubrication eventually made it easier for them to engage in intimacy. Emma entwined her legs around his waist as soft, alluring moans slipped from her lips. Her voice was incredibly beautiful, almost angelic.

William kept pushing himself deep inside her. Something brushed against the tip of his cock, causing him to feel it. It

Chapter One

must be her hymen he thought. He pushed himself relentlessly until she felt an extraordinary sensation, similar to an internal explosion. Emma screamed out loud and then smiled up at me. "Oh my! I just"

He was now drowning inside of her pool of honey. She was moving underneath him to his rhythm. They had become one. William was taken aback by the discovery of a woman who was both stunning and captivating. She was his soulmate.

"Oh, sweet Princess! Ahhhh! Mmmm f-feels good!" William cried out and began to tremble underneath her. Emma felt her pussy tighten around his cock as he neared climaxed. Emma then moved faster, and she too felt his balls boiling once again ready to shoot out his sperm. She tried to hold back but she felt so damn good. "Arrggghhh! I'm going to explode!" he cried out.

"Explode in me!" Emma pleaded.

William remained in her and felt long ropes of cum shooting so hard into his girl. She moaned louder. "I feel you! I feel you bursting in me!"

After shooting his last drop out, William moved back letting himself exit her. Emma looked up at her, puzzled. "Why didn't you stay in me?"

William blushed. "Because I'm finished."

Emma looked saddened. "I wanted you to stay in me forever. I'd never felt anything else more incredible sweet Duke."

He lay next to her, and she turned to face him. He touched her face as if he was some kind of dream. "This is the best night of my life," she said.

"Mine too."

Slowly they both drifted off into a deep sleep in each other's arms. They'd fallen for each other. Even though they were both

Forbidden Love

from two different worlds, their hearts belonged to each other.

III

The Island Princess by Kristin Boshears

The Dark Island

The Dark Island loomed ominously in the distance, shrouded in an eerie mist that clung to its jagged cliffs. The sea surrounding it seemed to murmur with an unsettling energy, as if whispering tales of the ill-fated vessels that had dared to approach its treacherous shores. James, a seasoned traveler with a rebellious spirit, felt a magnetic pull toward this enigmatic island. His boat, christened the "Wanderer," bobbed in the water, ready to embark on a journey that no one before had successfully completed.

As James finished gathering his belongings, he stole a glance at his parents standing on the balcony of their grand castle. King Richard, a stern but loving ruler watched with a mix of concern and fear. The king's aging eyes bore the weight of the crown, and he longed to see his family once again. James, however, craved the freedom of the open sea, an uncharted path that beckoned him beyond the realm of royal duties.

With a determined resolve, James waved farewell to his parents and stepped onto the creaking plank that connected the pier to his vessel. As he descended into the living quarters of the "Wanderer," he could feel the anticipation building within him. The captain, a weathered seafarer named Captain Morgan, welcomed James with a nod, his eyes reflecting a mixture of skepticism and curiosity.

James, tossing his bags onto the bed, took a seat and ran his fingers through his unruly black hair. In the dimly lit cabin, he joined the captain at the wooden table, surrounded by nautical maps and compasses. "So, boys, how long will it take for us to get there?" he asked with a casual air, trying to mask the gravity of the expedition ahead.

Captain Morgan squinted at the maps, tracing the perilous route with his calloused fingers. "A journey to the Dark Island ain't no Sunday sail, Your Highness," he replied, his voice tinged with a hint of caution. "We'll be navigatin' through unpredictable waters, and the winds, they dance to a mysterious tune around that cursed place. Can't rightly say how long it'll take, but we'll face whatever comes our way."

The crew, a motley bunch of sailors with weathered faces and tales of their own, listened intently as James and the captain discussed the uncertain voyage. The "Wanderer" creaked and swayed, ready to set sail into the unknown, as James and his crew prepared to challenge the mysteries that awaited them on the infamous Dark Island.

As the "Wanderer" set sail from the bustling harbor, the salty breeze carried the scent of adventure and uncertainty. The crew worked diligently, hoisting sails, and securing rigging, their movements synchronized like a well-practiced dance. James stood at the helm; his eyes fixed on the horizon where the Dark Island lurked like a mysterious specter. Captain Morgan joined him, squinting at the distant silhouette and offering a gruff

The Dark Island

reassurance, "We'll make it there, Your

Highness, but the sea can be a fickle mistress."

Days turned into nights, and the ship plowed through the undulating waves, leaving behind the familiar shores. The crew gathered on the deck, swapping stories of legendary sea creatures and recounting tales of those who dared to challenge the Dark Island. James, ever the curious soul, engaged in casual conversations with the sailors, learning about superstitions and maritime folklore. The camaraderie onboard eased the tension that clung to the air.

One evening, under a sky painted with hues of orange and pink, James found himself deep in conversation with the ship's navigator, a grizzled old sailor named Bartholomew. Leaning against the rail, Bartholomew spoke in hushed tones, sharing his own encounter with the mysterious island. "There be whispers, Your Highness," he confided, his eyes narrowing. "Whispers of voices carried by the wind, luring sailors into the heart of the unknown. But fear not, for we have your back."

The crew, a diverse mix of characters from all corners of the realm, developed a peculiar bond as they faced the challenges of the open sea. Laughter echoed across the deck during moments of respite, and even the creaks and groans of the ship seemed to join the lively symphony of camaraderie. James, despite his royal lineage, embraced the casual banter and shared meals with the crew, fostering a sense of unity among them.

As the "Wanderer" approached the vicinity of the Dark Island, an eerie stillness enveloped the sea. The crew exchanged wary glances, their usual banter replaced by solemn anticipation. James, sensing the shift in atmosphere, gathered the crew for a meeting on the deck. "We may be sailing into the unknown, my friends," he began, his voice carrying over the quiet sea, "but together, we shall face whatever challenges arise. Let's unlock the secrets of the Dark Island, not as individuals, but as a crew bound by a common purpose."

The crew nodded in agreement; their resolve strengthened by James's words. With the Dark Island looming ever closer, the "Wanderer" sailed onward, the crew and their royal passenger united by a shared quest for discovery. The sea whispered tales of the brave and the bold, and as the ship ventured into the mysterious waters, the journey to unravel the secrets of the Dark Island unfolded like a story waiting to be written.

High atop a rocky promontory on the Dark Island, overlooking the churning sea, stood a young woman named Seraphina. Her long, chestnut hair cascaded down her shoulders, catching the sunlight that managed to pierce through the heavy clouds overhead. Seraphina's caramel-toned skin spoke of a life spent beneath the sun's unyielding gaze. Her eyes, a deep shade of hazel, held a mixture of curiosity and suspicion as they fixed upon the approaching "Wanderer."

From her vantage point, she observed the ship with a furrowed brow, contemplating what manner of creature it might be. The waves splashed against the hull, and Seraphina's eyes widened with wonder. She pondered if it could be a massive sea creature, perhaps a new species unknown to her island. However, the absence of sharp teeth and the strange protrusions from its head left her baffled.

As the "Wanderer" drew closer, Seraphina's keen eyes detected movement on the ship. She squinted, trying to discern the nature of the smaller figure that emerged. To her amazement, it seemed to be a miniature version of the larger creature. A notion crossed her mind – was this a creature giving birth? The concept fascinated and perplexed her, prompting her to climb down from her rocky perch.

Gracefully navigating the dense foliage, Seraphina reached the shoreline just as the smaller creature made landfall. Clinging to the vines of a nearby tree, she peered down with a mix of astonishment and bewilderment. To her surprise, the smaller creature was not alone. It carried beings within it, creatures that resembled her own kind but seemed out of place. One among them looked significantly different, stirring a sense of curiosity and concern within Seraphina.

With a cautious approach, she observed the strangers, contemplating their presence on her secluded island. In a hushed voice, she muttered to herself, "What manner of beings are these, and why have they ventured into my home?" The unfolding mystery stirred a sense of protectiveness over her island sanctuary, and Seraphina remained concealed in the shadows, awaiting an opportune moment to unravel the secrets the "Wanderer" and its peculiar passengers held.

As Seraphina moved gracefully through the dense foliage, the vibrant emerald leaves rustled in response to her silent passage. The mysterious beings from the "Wanderer" continued their exploration of the island, unaware of the watchful eyes observing their every move. Seraphina, her lithe form blending seamlessly with the lush surroundings, sought a better vantage point to study the strangers and discern their intentions.

The one at the forefront of the group, James, ventured deeper into the wooded part of the island, his eyes wide with amazement at the unexplored beauty that unfolded before him. His footfalls were muffled by the thick carpet of moss beneath the towering trees. Meanwhile, Seraphina, her senses heightened, gripped onto branches and vines, concealing herself within the natural tapestry of the island.

Her attire, a simple arrangement of wraps that modestly covered her chest and waist, reflected a life untouched by the trappings of civilization. Seraphina had thrived on the bounty of the island, finding harmony in the untouched beauty that surrounded her. James, on the other hand, marveled at the unfamiliar flora and fauna, his expression a mix of awe and intrigue.

As the two worlds converged, Seraphina observed James with a mix of curiosity and wariness. She had never encountered outsiders on her secluded island, and the arrival of these strangers stirred a sense of protectiveness. James, captivated by the untouched paradise, ventured closer to where Seraphina concealed herself. Sensing an opportunity for communication, she emerged from the shadows, her presence revealed to James.

Their eyes met, hazel locking with a shade of blue, as both Seraphina and James stood on the precipice of an encounter that would unravel the mysteries of the Dark Island. The island, a silent witness to their meeting, held secrets that would soon be shared between its enigmatic guardian and the curious traveler from distant shores.

In the heart of the lush forest on the Dark Island, James James and Seraphina found themselves locked in a momentary gaze, each caught off guard by the other's presence. James, still in shock at the unexpected encounter, struggled to find words, while Seraphina's curiosity sparked a chain of thoughts in her hazel eyes. Suddenly, without a word, she reached above her head, her fingers curling around a lingering vine that dangled from the canopy above.

With a swift, agile movement, Seraphina yanked herself up into the trees, disappearing from James's view. Startled, he called out, "Hey, wait!" Ignoring the urgency in his voice,

The Dark Island

Seraphina maneuvered through the foliage with the grace of a woodland sprite, effortlessly leaping from branch to branch. James, driven by a mix of astonishment and determination, rushed after her, his footsteps echoing through the silent forest.

The forest seemed to come alive with the sound of rustling leaves and snapping twigs as the chase unfolded. Seraphina, navigating the treetops like a native bird, glanced back at James with a mischievous twinkle in her eyes. Unbeknownst to him, she was leading him through a labyrinth of ancient trees and hidden clearings, her actions fueled by a mysterious purpose.

As James continued to pursue the elusive figure, the forest around them transformed into a surreal landscape. The intertwining branches created a natural canopy overhead, filtering the sunlight into a mesmerizing dance of shadows. Seraphina's movements, guided by an innate connection to the land, guided James through a series of breathtaking vistas that revealed the untamed beauty of the Dark Island.

Despite the urgency of the chase, a silent understanding began to unfold between James and the island's guardian. In their pursuit, they entered a realm untouched by the passage of time, where the secrets of the Dark Island were whispered through the rustling leaves. The air crackled with an energy that hinted at an ancient connection between the mysterious girl and the enigmatic island they traversed together.

The clearing in the heart of the Dark Island's Forest became a stage for an unexpected encounter between James and Seraphina. As James cautiously approached, he sensed a certain tension in the air. With a gentle raising of his hands, he attempted to convey a message of peace to the mysterious girl. "Stay, please… I am not going to hurt you," he reassured, his voice carrying a sincerity that resonated through the tranquil

Forbidden Love

glade.

Seraphina regarded James with a mixture of curiosity and wariness. The forest seemed to hold its breath as a massive wolf, as tall as Seraphina herself, emerged from the shadows. The creature, a majestic Timber wolf with fur the color of rich earth, exuded an aura of ancient wisdom. However, this was no ordinary wolf; it was a dire wolf, a creature of legend known for its size and strength. James, his eyes widening in disbelief, desperately sought to convey his peaceful intentions to both the girl and her formidable companion.

The tension in the clearing reached its peak as James faced the imposing dire wolf. Yet, to his surprise, the creature emitted a huff and turned away, vanishing into the depths of the forest.

James, still catching his breath, looked up at Seraphina with a mixture of awe and confusion. "W…who are you?" he stammered, captivated by the enigma that surrounded her.

For a moment, Seraphina's hazel eyes mirrored his confusion. Then, with a simple yet profound response, she uttered, "I don't know." The words hung in the air, leaving an air of mystery between them. The Dark Island, with its ancient secrets and mystical inhabitants, seemed to conspire in the unfolding of a tale that bound a curious James and an enigmatic guardian, both drawn into the embrace of the island's timeless mysteries.

As Seraphina led James through the intricate labyrinth of the Dark Island's Forest, the foliage embraced them like a living tapestry. The verdant greenery seemed to form a barrier, shielding their clandestine journey from prying eyes. James, not accustomed to such wild terrain, struggled to keep pace with the agile girl. "Wait! You're going too fast!" he called out, his breath labored as they traversed the uneven ground.

Seraphina, however, moved through the forest with an

The Dark Island

effortless grace, her lithe form navigating the treetops and vines as if part of the natural dance of the island. After a series of swift movements, they arrived at a secluded spot where the forest canopy gave way to a hidden treehouse. The makeshift home stood among the ancient branches, constructed from wood salvaged from the wrecks of ships that had met their fate on the island's treacherous shores.

Breathing heavily, James marveled at the ingenuity of Seraphina's refuge. The treehouse was a sanctuary woven from the remnants of the outside world, with furniture crafted from the debris of crashed ships. As James explored the intricacies of the treehouse, the wooden structure creaked beneath their weight, creating a symphony of sounds that resonated through the forest.

"Uh, we are safe here, right?" James inquired, glancing at the wooden planks beneath him. Seraphina, looking down at him from her elevated perch, simply uttered, "Safe." Her assurance brought a sense of comfort to James, who nodded in gratitude. His eyes wandered, taking in the simplicity and depth of the treehouse. As he strolled around, he noticed a collection of suitcases, each adorned with a family crest indicating their royal origins.

Curiosity piqued; James approached the suitcases. Opening one, he discovered regal garments and items adorned with insignias of noble houses. The revelation sparked a realization – the remnants of past shipwrecks had brought not only debris but also travelers from royal families who had sought refuge on the mysterious Dark Island. The treehouse, a haven nestled among the ancient branches, held secrets that transcended the boundaries of time and royalty.

In the tranquil seclusion of the Dark Island's treehouse, James and Seraphina found themselves surrounded by the remnants of royal travelers who sought refuge on the enigmatic island. As James inspected the suitcases, his eyes were drawn to a particular one that had seen better days. Seraphina, watching his every move with keen interest, approached him and gently picked up the faded suitcase, worn down by the passage of time. The once vibrant royal blue had transformed into a murky gray-blue, and the case itself was on the brink of deterioration.

With a simplicity that spoke volumes, Seraphina declared, "Mine," handing James the fragile artifact of a bygone era. His fingers traced the golden dragon emblem on the case, a symbol of a noble lineage. The revelation left James wide-eyed with astonishment. "Wait, this is a royal family crest," he exclaimed, his gaze fixed on the mysterious girl before him. Doubt and disbelief flickered across his face as he questioned, "Are you sure this is yours?"

Seraphina, with a slow nod as if retrieving fragments of a distant memory, affirmed her connection to the worn suitcase. In that moment, James's perspective shifted. Rising to his feet, he seized Seraphina's hands, a gesture that made her flinch. "Come with me, come back with me, I mean… Your family has been looking for you since the crash!" he implored urgently, his voice filled with a newfound determination to reunite her with her kin.

However, Seraphina, shaking her head with a gentle resolve, uttered, "Home, this is my home." James, sensing the complexity of her emotions, persisted, "No, I know, but you have another home with a family!" The unfolding conversation took an unexpected turn as Seraphina questioned, "What of Star?" The mention of the wolf prompted a nervous chuckle from James, who fumbled over his words before admitting, "Uh…I… Uh…

The Dark Island

hm."

The awkward pause that followed hinted at the unspoken understanding – Star, the majestic dire wolf, would accompany Seraphina. The bond between the guardian of the Dark Island and her formidable companion was unbreakable. James, now torn between the allure of the island and the desire to reunite Seraphina with her family, grappled with the complexities of their shared journey. The treehouse, with its collection of memories and revelations, became a nexus of decisions that would shape the destinies of James, the mysterious girl, and the island itself.

The "Wanderer" returned to the boat docks sooner than expected, and confusion rippled through the crew. The sailors, still grappling with the abrupt end to their journey, exchanged bewildered glances and whispered questions about whether they had even reached the infamous Dark Island. Among the queries, the identity of the mysterious girl and the colossal wolf accompanying her became the focal point of speculation.

James, however, had a singular purpose – to shield Seraphina from the prying eyes of the curious onlookers. The wolf, with its towering presence, sent shockwaves through the crowd. Panic ensued as sailors jumped off the docking ports and others fled in a frenzy, startled by the sight of the massive creature. The dire wolf, undeterred by the chaos, remained close to Seraphina's side, casting an image of an oversized, albeit gentle, lost puppy.

With a determined stride, James led Seraphina away from the chaos, guiding her through the bustling harbor. His stern expression warned off anyone who dared to question or interfere. The city streets became a maze of curious glances and hushed whispers as the unusual trio made their way towards the royal palace.

As they approached the grand gates of the palace, the guards, initially taken aback by the sight of the wolf, hastily opened them upon recognizing James. The trio entered the palace grounds, leaving behind the clamor of the docks. James, mindful of the gazes lingering on Seraphina and the wolf, guided her with a protective presence.

Once inside the palace, away from the prying eyes of the public, James addressed Seraphina, his voice a low murmur, "We'll find a way to keep Star here safe and secure. You're home now, and we'll figure everything out together." The palace, with its ornate halls and majestic corridors, became the backdrop for a new chapter in Seraphina's life, intertwined with the destinies of the Dark Island, the royal family, and the enigmatic guardian who had found a home in unexpected places.

The palace halls buzzed with whispered curiosity as James, Seraphina, and the formidable dire wolf entered the royal grounds. Eager to keep the mysterious trio away from the prying eyes of the public, James guided them through the lavish corridors and opulent chambers. The wolf, its imposing figure a stark contrast to the regal surroundings, remained dutifully at Seraphina's side.

As they reached the heart of the palace, James took a moment to confer with a maid and a guard. Urgency marked his voice as he explained the situation, the maid's eyes widening in shock. She exchanged a quick glance with the guard, and a shared understanding passed between them. "We must tell the king, but first, let's get her cleaned up," the maid declared, motioning for others to join them.

A group of maids and guards assembled, ready to assist in tending to Seraphina's needs. The maid, taking charge,

The Dark Island

approached the enigmatic girl with a gentle demeanor. "Come, my dear, we'll make sure you're comfortable and clean," she assured, guiding Seraphina away to a chamber prepared for such occasions. The palace, with its grandeur and intricate details, now bore witness to a peculiar union of worlds – the untamed mystique of the Dark Island brought into the heart of royal opulence.

In the designated chamber, Seraphina was treated with care by the attending maids. The gentle rustle of silken fabrics mingled with the splashing of water as they worked to cleanse away the traces of the island's wilderness. The atmosphere, though adorned with the elegance of the palace, carried a sense of shared humanity as the maids tended to Seraphina's needs.

After the cleansing rituals, the girl emerged, adorned in a simple yet elegant gown provided by the palace. Her caramel-toned skin glowed, and her eyes sparkled with a newfound radiance. James, observing the transformation, felt a swell of pride at having played a part in bringing her from the untamed beauty of the Dark Island to the refined splendor of the royal palace. The story of Seraphina, the guardian of the island, had now become intricately woven into the fabric of royal court life, ready to unfold in unexpected ways.

The palace's lavish chamber transformed into a sanctuary of grace and tenderness as Seraphina underwent the ritual of cleansing and adorning. The maids, with gentle hands and compassionate hearts, led her into a luxuriously appointed bathroom adorned with ornate mirrors and glistening marble. The scent of fragrant oils and blossoms filled the air as the maids carefully undressed her, revealing a layer of dirt and remnants from her life on the Dark Island.

In the soothing warmth of the bath, the maids diligently

washed away the traces of wilderness, whispering comforting words as they combed through Seraphina's tangled hair. The warm water cascaded over her, carrying with it the weight of her solitary existence on the secluded island. The maids, recognizing the profound significance of this moment, approached their task with a delicate reverence, treating Seraphina not just as a visitor but as a lost member of their own kin.

After the cleansing ritual, the maids wrapped her in luxurious towels, their softness a stark contrast to the harshness of her previous life. They carefully brushed her hair, untangling each strand with patience and care. The transformation was gradual but profound, as the dirt and weariness gave way to a radiant beauty that had been hidden beneath the wilderness.

Once the grooming was complete, Seraphina was presented with a royal blue gown that sparkled and shined under the palace's ambient lights. Matching shoes adorned her feet, and her hair, now a cascade of bouncy curls, framed her face like a crown. The transformation was complete, revealing a beauty that transcended the confines of the Dark Island.

As she stepped out of the bathroom, James, overwhelmed by the enchanting vision before him, escorted her alongside the guards toward the throne room. The anticipation hung in the air as they approached the king, whose back was turned to them. The guard cleared his throat, drawing the king's attention. Before the king could utter a word, his gaze met Seraphina's.

Time seemed to stand still as recognition flickered in the king's eyes. The few items he held dropped to the floor, forgotten, as he descended the steps toward his long-lost daughter. Tears welled in his eyes as he reached out to cup Seraphina's cheeks, his voice choked with emotion. James,

The Dark Island

respecting the sacredness of the moment, discreetly stepped back, allowing the father and daughter to embrace the reunion that had transcended time and distance. The throne room, witness to countless tales of joy and sorrow, now cradled a moment that resonated with the poignant beauty of family reunited against all odds.

Three years had passed since the emotional reunion between King Reginald and his long-lost daughter, Seraphina. In that time, the palace had witnessed a transformation, not just in the physical appearance of the once wild and solitary guardian of the Dark Island, but in the very fabric of the kingdom's heart. Love had blossomed unexpectedly between James James and Seraphina, defying the boundaries of social status and the mysteries of their divergent pasts.

As the sun dipped below the horizon, casting a warm glow over the royal gardens adorned with vibrant blossoms, the palace grounds were abuzz with anticipation. The air was filled with the sweet melodies of songbirds, echoing the joyous notes of the impending union. The grandeur of the ceremony spoke to the resilience of love that had weathered the storms of uncertainty.

In the opulent throne room, adorned with rich tapestries and flickering candlelight, James James, now a beloved figure of the kingdom, awaited Seraphina at the altar. Her royal blue gown, reminiscent of the dress she wore on the day of her rediscovery, shimmered with an ethereal grace. The scent of flowers filled the air as Seraphina walked down the aisle, a radiant vision of love and redemption.

The ceremony, officiated by the palace priest, unfolded with solemn vows and promises exchanged between James and Seraphina. The echoes of their heartfelt words reverberated through the hall, a testament to the resilience of love that had bridged the gap between two worlds. As they exchanged rings, the golden bands became symbols not only of their commitment but also of the unity forged from the tapestry of their intertwined destinies.

The gathered nobles and commoners alike bore witness to the union that defied expectations and norms. Tears of joy and awe glistened in the eyes of those present, moved by the profound beauty of the love that had triumphed over adversity. King Reginald, standing proudly by his daughter's side, beamed with happiness as he handed her over to James, signifying the continuation of their intertwined journey.

In the closing moments of the ceremony, as the newlyweds shared their first dance beneath the palace's grand chandeliers, a profound truth resonated. Love, in its purest form, knows no boundaries. It doesn't discriminate based on background, family, or circumstance. It says yes to the union of two souls, weaving a tapestry that transcends the limitations of the world. The kingdom, now united not only by blood but by love, stood witness to a love story that would echo through the annals of time, reminding all who heard it that love's magic knows no preferences – it simply says yes.

IV

The Protectors by Maria Marandola

A Warm Welcome Back

The dead bird lying at her feet had to be a bad omen - especially in a graveyard.

Rapunzel stared at her mother's tombstone - tears didn't come as easily anymore but the emptiness she felt inside was still deep as ever. She swept her long golden braids over her shoulder and crouched down. She rummaged through her travel bag, looking for the gift she brought back for her mother, an emerald green scarf with silver stars. She gently wrapped the bird in it, and placed it on the grave. An offering.

"The colors reminded me of you." She sighed and traced the etchings of her parents' names.

Joseph & Solaria Thorne

Her father wasn't buried there. He left for war and never returned. Rapunzel barely remembers him it was so long ago. At least this way, they could be together in death, even if only symbolically. She brushed the tears that managed to escape away. Her first stop whenever she came back home and always the hardest.

Forbidden Love

The graveyard was adjacent to the only church is Oakwood and on the outskirts of town. Rapunzel imagined walking the tree-lined path from the church to the center of town as a parade. As much as she loved being out seeing the world and discovering new things, the warmth of comfort of being back home was always welcome.

At least until I remember nothing is the same anymore.

The weathered wooden sign of The Cozy Duckling swung lazily from rusted iron chains. A duck tucked into a nest was carved under faded purple lettering. The tavern, the first in Avalonia, was covered in long vines of ivy with painted wooden shutters on the small square windows. It was also Rapunzel's home when she wasn't on the road.

The smell of fresh bread beckoned her inside. Her stomach churned as she crossed the threshold. The roaring fire in the stone fireplace warmed her wind-blown cheeks. The slow strumming of a lute added a festive atmosphere to the general din of conversation. While parents chatted about the weather, Avalonia, or the price of food, their children played together by the fire.

A small body slammed into Rapunzel's left leg as the baker's son jumped into her arms for a hug. She stumbled, almost falling backward.

"Rapunzel! Do you have a story for me?" His eyes shone with curiosity, mirroring her own youthful dreams. The wooden sword his father carved for him hung from his back in a handmade sheath.

"I might, but it'll have to wait until I eat something," she responded, rustling his unruly curls. "I just got back."

"Oh, okay" His shoulders slumped, a frown forming. She sighed; he knew she couldn't resist that look.

A Warm Welcome Back

" Eli, I promise next time I'll tell you about when I defeated a three-headed water serpent."

"Did you use your hair to tie it up before slicing off its heads?" he asked, eyes wide, swinging his sword.

"You'll have to wait to find out." She winked.

He ran to his mother and catapulted into her arms. She raised her eyes and gave Rapunzel a beaming smile and a welcoming wave. Her wild curls peeped out from under her bonnet even as she tried to tuck them away. Rapunzel laughed in understanding. Her own braids a constant obstacle.

Rapunzel walked up to Martha, the owner of the tavern, and her surrogate family. She swept the floor, her graying hair coming loose from her low bun. Rapunzel embraced her tightly.

"Rapunzel, I'm so glad you're back."

"I'm glad to see you, too. I have a gift for you, but after I eat."

Martha chuckled. "Artemus is at the table."

"Thank you, Martha. Bring me whatever he ordered, if you don't mind?"

Martha nodded and walked back to the kitchen, broom in hand.

Artemus sat at their usual table near the window. He was hunched over his journal, the sun highlight the red in his chestnut locs, his brow furrowed. He pinched the bridge of his nose with his left hand, deep in thought. He brushed a few errant twists out of his eyes before taking a long sip of his half-empty mug.

"Everything okay?" Rapunzel asked as she sat across from him.

"King Magnus is dead." His deep voice husky with emotion.

"That's terrible. When did it happen?" Rapunzel remembered the king fondly. She and Artemus spent a lot of time at the palace as children, with the prince, Leander. That's how she and Artemus met. While their parents worked, they would amuse themselves with endless games.

"Last night. Marcel told me at the market." He rubbed the back of his neck and finished the last of his ale.

"Wasn't he sick?"

He nodded. "Nobody here knows. They haven't sent word to the villages yet."

They grew silent when Martha approached. Her tray was loaded with two mugs of her famous honey mead and two steaming bowls of beef stew. She placed everything on the table, patted Rapunzel's shoulder lovingly, and walked away.

"How is the Queen handling it? And Leander, does he know?"

"I heard Leander wasn't living at the palace anymore because of the wicked stepmother," he whispered, a devious glint in his sapphire eyes. He wasn't normally one to spread gossip, but neither of them liked Morgana.

Morgana was the reason they stopped going to the palace. The day she dismissed Theron and Solaria, along with some others, they never went back. She had only seen Leander one time after that, on her 16th birthday.

"A toast to King Magnus?" Rapunzel asked, eyebrow cocked, and glass raised. They clinked their mugs together.

"To King Magnus, a fair ruler who will be missed." They each took a big swig of their drinks before digging into their meal.

They savored the aroma of fresh herbs and spices which gave the stew a hearty taste. Martha's meals always welcomed them home. Artemus grabbed the last piece of crusty bread from the basket.

"Where to next, Artemus? I believe it's your turn to pick." They didn't stay in Oakwood very long, after a week they were

A Warm Welcome Back

usually itching to get back on the road. The pain felt deeper here, it was harder to pretend everything was normal.

"There's a village by the Nordhaven Sea – I've read stories of a sea dragon and artifacts used for hunting them."

"The sea again? That serpent on the last sea voyage almost roasted us!"

Artemus looked up from his stew, the sopping bread halfway between the bowl and his mouth. His gaze locked with hers, the intensity of his stare sending her stomach fluttering.

"You know I won't let anything roast us. Besides, your hair gets us out of trouble every time, if my arrows don't."

Only when she could control it. She toyed with the ends of one of her braids. She couldn't imagine life without her mysterious hair anymore. It was a constant reminder of her mother, a constant reminder of the power that flowed within her, if only she knew how to unlock it. Solaria transferred her powers to Rapunzel moments before her death. However, the magic only manifested in her hair. It grew seven feet long, which is why she kept it in four thick braids that hung down her back.

At least Artemus got something useful from his father before he died. An ornately carved bow that depicted images of little hunters in the woods, and enchanted arrows for killing magical creatures. His dad only had two arrows left; he had used when before Artemus was born. While he used the bow all the time, the arrows were "emergency only".

"Well, me and my hair were thinking something new and different. Maybe the desert. It would be a longer trip, but I think we could manage."

"Not a bad idea, maybe you could finally get some color." He winked and finished the last of his stew, using the crust as a spoon.

"We can't all be as lucky as you." She quipped.

They debated the pros and cons of each location, other patrons interrupting them to say hello or ask what items we might have for sale. Whatever we brought back, we bartered for goods or money with shopkeepers all over Avalonia. When everything was gone, we used the money made to fund our next adventure.

"Excuse me, ma'am…" Rapunzel turned in her seat. She hadn't seen the King's sage, Alderwick, since her mother was alive, but there he was. His hair, once salt & pepper had turned snowy white a stark contrast to his golden brown skin. He was tall and slim, although the robes he wore added bulk to his frame. Next to him was Finn Silverwind, the King's bard.

Martha pointed in our direction.

"Artemus, do you see Alderwick and Finn coming our way, or have I had too much mead?" she asked. She lifted her hand slowly to wave.

"They are there, but why?" He squinted and raised his eyebrow dramatically. Rapunzel stifled a laugh.

"The King." She mouthed to him right before Finn and Alderwick approached. His eyes widened.

"Rapunzel, Artemus, I'm glad I found you here. I was worried I came all this way for nothing," Alderwick greeted.

"Alderwick! Finn!" Rapunzel shouted enthusiastically. "What brings you all this way to look for us?"

"If it's about King Magnus, we already know. My condolences to Morgana and Leander," Artemus said.

"I wish that were all. Prince Leander is missing."

Rapunzel's eyes opened wide in surprise and she gasped. Missing? Rapunzel calmed herself, not wanting to draw any

A Warm Welcome Back

more attention than Alderwick's arrival already had. If the villagers didn't know the King had died yet, they certainly didn't know this.

"Is there somewhere else we can go to speak? Somewhere more private?" he asked.

Artemus and Rapunzel glanced at each other; confusion mirrored in each other's eyes. Artemus nodded, walked over to Martha. Martha nodded, and Artemus waved them over. He led them through the kitchen and down the steps to the cellar.

"Missing? Since when?" Rapunzel fired off her questions as soon as they were alone.

"Morgana had sent word for him a week ago to come and see his father. He should have arrived yesterday morning, but he didn't." Alderwick's voice was laden with sadness. He had worked with the King a long time.

"A hunter found the guard's body near the road," Finn explained.

"I"m sorry to hear that, but I don't understand why you're here?" Rapunzel asked.

Alderwick and Finn locked eyes, confusing Rapunzel. Artemus leaned against a pillar, arms crossed in front of him. His indifference was a complete pivot to Rapunzel's frazzled nerves. She wished they would just get to the point.

"I came to you because of your gift. It can help." His gaze shifted to the long braids trailing down Rapunzel's back. She instinctively reached for them, unsure why they'd play a part in finding the prince.

"I can't control it. My mother didn't have a chance to show me." A tear zigzagged down her cheek, and Artemus stepped closer to the three of them.

"I can teach you."

Rapunzel hesitated; she hadn't seen Leander since the night of her sixteenth birthday. When he snuck out beyond the Palace walls to celebrate with her: just the two of them. Even now, she could feel his smooth hands running up and down the soft skin of her back.

"Can we talk further about this after the tavern closes?" Alderwick asked, snapping Rapunzel out of her daydream.

Artemus nodded, knowing Martha would agree. "Be here at nine o'clock. Everyone will be gone by then."

"Great. I have some business to attend to at the herbalist shop, and Finn needs to inform folks of the King's passing. We will see you this evening."

Alderwick and Finn went back upstairs. Artemus stayed silent until we could no longer hear their footsteps.

"Zel," he began, using her childhood nickname, "do you trust them?"

"We can hear what he says, can't we?" The thought of learning more about the power she possessed was appealing. If that meant she had to help him in return, it might be worth it.

He paced back and forth. "Is there anything else?" she asked. She hated when he wouldn't just say what was on his mind.

"Would you do it for me?" he asked, longing in his voice.

"Why would you ask me that?" She was frozen in place, trying to surprise the overwhelming urge to slap him.

"You told me how hard it was when you never saw him again. How in love you were with him?"

"I shared that with you as a friend, not for you to use it to mock me."

She pivoted on her heel and ran up the stairs. She fumed silently in the kitchen, allowing herself a moment to calm down. She had just been reminiscing about his touch, had her face

A Warm Welcome Back

given something away.

"Zel, I'm sorry. I shouldn't have said that." Her approached her with his hands raised in a peace offering.

"No, you shouldn't have," she snipped.

"So, does that mean you do prefer my company," he whispered, moving in closer, a grin on his face. "Because our last evening together in our tent tells me you might."

She groaned, his lips on the edge of her earlobe.

"Barely." Her arms were crossed tightly under her breasts. She shoved him away forcefully. "What if Martha sees, she'll think something is going on."

"Something is going on, even if it is only a casual arrangement between friends, as you so lovingly put it," he teased.

"You know how I feel about that," she countered. This conversation had come up twice during their last trip. Him convincing her they should be more, and her hesitant to take that plunge with him. What if it didn't work out, what if she lost him forever?

"Oh, I know," he said, pulling her closer. He planted his lips against her ear; he knew what those whispers did to her.

"Artemus, stop!" Rapunzel shoved him away, and he dramatically fell backward, clutching his heart with his hands.

Rapunzel rolled her eyes, but a small smile sneaked its way onto her face. She wished she could trust how they felt about each other, and she did, when she thought they both wanted the same thing.

"Let's go see what we supplies we can trade or sell before this evening," Rapunzel suggested.

"Excellent idea! I'll meet you out front shortly. I have to finish my notes."

As he walked away, questions zipped through her mind. Was

their casual arrangement on the road, turning into something more? That wasn't what they agreed to. And did she still have feelings for Leander after all these years apart? But those phantom hands on her hips sent shivers up her spine every time. She shook the thoughts from her head before heading out to get ready to sweet-talk the shop owners.

A Missing Prince

The fire crackled loudly. They sat at the table and helped themselves to drinks while they waited. By the time they met earlier, the word of the King's passing had started to spread. Many of the older residents walked around with long faces, each wanting to reminisce about the king. When they returned to the tavern, they were exhausted from the emotional impact of the day.

"I saw a dead bird this morning. What do you think that means?"

"I think that means this needs to be a joint decision, Zel. You can't let him play on your emotions."

"That's not what it means. Besides, we don't need to do everything together."

His face fell at the suggestion, but that didn't really sound appealing to her, either.

The door swung open, bringing in the night breeze with it. Her comment was left dangling between them. Alderwick and Finn joined them at the table, the tension of the day etched on their weary faces.

"It's important this information stays between us," Alderwick began, placing his palms on the table.

Finn leaned back in his chair, his eyes closed. She wondered briefly what his part in this was and why he was privy to private information.

"Of course," Rapunzel replied. Artemus shrugged his shoulders, a scowl etched into his face.

"Artemus, did your father leave you anything when he passed?"

Artemus' body tensed. "Yes, his bow, quiver, and a couple of enchanted arrows." At least this wasn't only about her now.

"Did he ever explain why?"

"It was a heirloom, his great-grandfather carved it himself. I never asked about the arrows though."

He nodded and pulled out a map, spreading it on the table. A journal also materialized from his large bag, tattered and worn with time and use.

Rapunzel inspected the map, faded lines and symbols, marked roads, landmarks, and other small villages in the kingdom, along with the woods surrounding them. It was in the patch of green that Rapunzel noticed a circle along the road. Around that circle was a larger one.

Alderwick tapped the inner circle. "This is where the driver was found." His eyes gleamed in the light of the fire, and he tapped the outer circle. "This is where we think he might be, based on when he was supposed to arrive and when we found the guard."

"Those woods are full of hunters shacks, cottages, and caves," Artemus said.

"They are, but only one of those places is Morgana's family

A Missing Prince

home, the Darkspire Manor. It's long been abandoned but still belongs to her."

"You don't think she would-?" Rapunzel had heard terrible things about Morgana over the years, but this seemed extreme. What did they have to do with any of this?

"And what do my bow and arrows and Rapunzel's hair have to do with this?" Artemus asked, reading her mind.

He leaned forward, his broad shoulders straining against his coat.

"The Darkspire's have attempted to claim Avalonia for themselves for generations. Theron and Solaria were a part of that history and now the two of you are as well."

Rapunzel's mouth hung open; she couldn't believe this. How could her mother not tell her this before she died.

"The Protectors. A hunter, a sage, and a sorceress." Rapunzel blinked, a sorceress, a protector. Not possible. She wasn't capable. She could barely protect herself.

Artemus shook his head and locked eyes with Rapunzel. She shrugged, just as confused as he looked.

"Will you help us?" Artemus asked, "since you are the sage in this little trio of heroes."

"I wish I could be by your side, but I can't do anything out of the ordinary. She's always been suspicious of me. Finn is my protege, unbeknownst to Morgana." He motioned toward Finn who sat up straighter at the mention of his name. "He will accompany you when the time comes, but first you must find the prince."

He tapped the journal. "This has a lot of information, about your roles, and all I know about Morgana."

"All you know?" Rapunzel asked. "What more is there?"

"You'll see. I only wish we realized who she was before he

married her." He dropped his head, looking every bit his age in that moment.

Rapunzel traced the journal's emblem: a bow with a sun in its center, and a vine weaving its way around the bow. "What is this symbol?"

"It's the seal of the protectors."

"What does this mean for us?" Artemus asked.

"It means you need to be careful," Finn interjected. "People will be looking for you."

"Can we have a moment to discuss this?"

"Of course," Alderwick replied, "but time is of the essence."

artemus led Rapunzel to the kitchen and spun around to face her.

"Do we really want to do this? Do we really want us to venture into this unknown situation…for him?" Artemus asked, arms thrown in the air.

"Not for him…," she began. "But what if Morgana is planning something terrible?"

His gaze softened. "Zel, we can't save the whole world."

"I'm not asking for that. I'm asking for you to care about Martha, Eli and his family, Joseph, Luke, and all the other people in Oakwood."

He clenched his jaw, closed his eyes, and took a deep breath.

"You're infuriating sometimes, Zel. I don't know why you care so much about a place that turned its back on us."

A discussion they've had many times before. Her always wanting to go back to Oakwood instead of seeing where their adventures could take them. Where he wanted to plunge forward into the unknown, she wanted to hang on to memories and happier times.

Instead of making my own happier times.

A Missing Prince

"Don't you want to understand? Find out the truth?"

"Not really. I don't really want to learn why I'm destined to protect Leander for the rest of my life."

"I do. Not protect him but finally figure out the purpose of this," she said flipping her braids in the air. They swung up and back down around her like a cape.

"Fine, we can do this, since it's important for you, but what about when we're done?"

"What do you mean?" Rapunzel crossed her arms and glared at him through squinted eyes.

"I mean if I say I'm ready to move on from Oakwood, from Avalonia, will you consider coming with me…forever?"

Rapunzel squirmed under the weight of "forever". What if it didn't work out? She'd be far from home without no one but her thoughts to drive her crazy.

"I don't want to say yes right now, because I'm not sure. But… if you choose to leave after we're done I won't try to stop you." He didn't deserve her holding him back with her uncertainty.

He nodded and they informed Alderwick and Finnian that they'd leave first thing in the morning.

"Thank you. I am leaving you with the journal and map. And a bit of sleeping tonic just in case you need a hand," he winked, the shadows lifted from his face with their agreement to help.

Rapunzel and Leander huddled close together after the pair left. The journal was open on the table between them, the quiet of the tavern creating an intimate moment, like on their trips.

They pored over the pages, pages of Alderwick's handwritten notes. Suspicions, questions, tidbits of research. Their arms and legs constantly brushing against each other. Their rhythm once again in sync.

"Look here," Rapunzel said, pointing to an entry dated three months before the King's death, in Alderwick's neat print. *Magnus was healthy just last month, what could have made his health decline so quickly? Did Morgana do something?*

"Do you really think he has proof?" Artemus asked. "What if he's involved in all this and just needs us dead?" Rapunzel raised her eyebrows and shook her head. Artemus and his wild theories.

Rapunzel took a deep, steadying breath and met his gaze. Some of the truth will never be discovered, but why would Alderwick give them this information? Why not just kill them?

"I don't think Alderwick is involved," she replied. "But this journal can give us some insight." All the information she never received, the magic she never learned.

Their eyes still locked, he sighed. "It seems like it's our problem then, no matter what."

"We'll be careful, like we always are." She laughed, knowing that they weren't always careful, but at least they had each other's back.

"When should we leave? It'll take the better part of the day just to get through the kingdom to the edge of the forest.

"Let's leave in the morning, after breakfast. We can camp when we reach the forest. We'll stop for a new tent and extra supplies along the way, since that wolf ruined the last one."

"The journey is the part I'm least worried about, Zel. Stop overplanning, when has that ever worked for you?" he chuckled. "I just don't understand why they didn't tell us before they died?"

The familiarity of this moment wasn't lost on Rapunzel. Reassurances to each other before another adventure. Concerns and fears shared. This time was different - saving a life and an entire kingdom was a far cry from hunting for treasure. artemus squeezed Rapunzel's hand, the warmth matching that of the fire and waking up her senses. She pushed the feelings stirring in her aside. Normally, it would wait until they were tucked in together in a tent. Huddled together for warmth, she'd reach down and –

She stopped that thought in its tracks before she invited him into her bed, her bed was definitely off-limits.

"I'm going to try to get some sleep. You should too."

She slid the chair away. He tugged her hand and pressed his lips to her knuckles. She melted inside.

"Artemus," she whispered. "It's time for me to go to bed."

He released her hand and smiled. "We ride at dawn!" Rapunzel chuckled before heading to her room.

She laid in bed, eyes shut but her mind was in overdrive. Did Alderwick have all the facts? Were they putting themselves in danger they didn't understand. That was something they always did but at least that was for themselves.

Rapunzel gave up on trying to sleep and rose before the sun. She flipped through the pages of the journal, unable to read it in the dark, but its brittle pages offering her comfort. Something caught her eye. She sat up and held the book up to her face, a water lily on the top of a page in gold ink. She noticed the entire page was written using the gold ink that shimmered in the faint moonlight, in her mother's girlish script.

The Water Lily: Magic of the Sun

She recognized the lyrics to the song her mother used to sing to her. She would sing it before bedtime, but she remembered her singing it when she scraped her knee or bumped her shin. She would bandage the wound and sing the song. She traced her fingers over the words, a tear landed on her hand, and she wiped it on the blanket and closed the journal.

Her beige tunic hung loosely around her slender curves as

she repacked her bag. She gathered clothes, her brush, ribbons for her hair, her compass, her travel journal, along with the map and book Alderwick provided them. She slipped on brown leather pants that fit like a second skin. A corset loosely tied around her waist gave most men the impression she was harmless, without suspecting it was where she hid her daggers.

The courageous adventurer in the mirror was born from tragedy and necessity, but she couldn't help but wonder. What would her life be like if the dreams and wishes she and Leander whispered to each other in that tower came true? She never thought herself a princess but for him she would have.

She closed her eyes and took a deep breath. The words to the song were floating in her head and she softly began singing it. The air around her started to crackle with energy, she opened her eyes, and her golden air was shimmering the way the words on the page did. She gasped and stopped singing, her hair fading back to strawberry blonde.

"Well, that's a start," she said to her reflection. She slung her quiver over her shoulder, grabbed her bow and her bag, then headed out the door.

Martha was already downstairs, the first batch of bread coming out of the oven. She took one look at Rapunzel, and her face fell.

"You're leaving again so soon? But the King's funeral, the mourning period," Martha pleaded, having been a mess since she heard.

"I'm sorry. I wouldn't go if it weren't important." Rapunzel wrapped a comforting arm around her and slid a small package in front of her.

"What's this?"

"Your gift."

A Missing Prince

Martha slowly unwrapped the package, and pulled out the bonnet Rapunzel picked up at a tiny shop. It was blue with white lace trim.

"It's lovely." She rewrapped it and placed it aside. "At least let me pack you some food." She filled a large burlap sack with three loaves of fresh bed, a satchel of olives, apples, pears. She added some dried meats and nuts on the top.

"Thank you, Martha."

Martha nodded sadly. "Be safe."

Artemus entered the kitchen as they were ending their goodbye. He hugged Martha just as tightly. They were a family born of tragedy, but a family, nonetheless.

They stepped out into the early morning – Rapunzel took a moment to breathe in the fresh air. When she opened her eyes, Artemus' gaze was focused on her. She should tell him what she discovered? Not yet, not in the village. She would wait until they were alone and safe.

"I love that you do that every time we leave," he said.

Her cheeks warmed under the glow of his adoration. It was easy to see why she was so confused these days. Artemus was the last thread of who she was, to lose him because of foolish passion that would fizzle was not an option. It was better for her to keep him at arm's length.

She pulled the map out of her bag. "We should get to the forest entry behind the palace by nightfall."

"We'll stop along the way to trade. I still have some of the tools we found on the last trip, and you have the fur from that wolf that almost got us."

"Because someone fell asleep on their watch," Rapunzel replied, pointedly.

When they arrived at the drawbridge leading to the palace,

they decided to pay a visit to Marcel. They crossed the solid oak bridge, secured with large iron chains. The guards nodded as we passed. The atmosphere around town was heavy with grief. Most of the shops were closed to pay respects to their lost king. The few that were open for necessities, had lanterns out in front with large displays of flowers, coins, bottles of spirits, and candies.

The people who were out, kept their heads down and voices low.

"Let's just do what we have to and get out of here," Rapunzel whispered. "I feel like we're trespassing."

"We'll be quick. We should get camp setup before the sun goes down completely anyway."

Despite the somber mood, Marcel was ever the salesman. He greeted them with staged enthusiasm and happily traded the wolf pelt for a tent and rope. They left the town and crossed back over the bridge, the palace the perfect backdrop to their exit.

The Journey

The next morning, Artemus' movements around the tent woke her. She lifted herself up on her elbows, the throbbing in her head reminding her they had one too many cups of Martha's mead before settling in for the night.

She watched Artemus move around hurriedly, the events of the evening a blur, but she remembered feeling his body curled up against hers, his breath hot on her neck. Why did this always happen? The lines were getting too blurred between them.

"Why don't you ever wake me?" she asked.

"I tried, but you couldn't hear me over all your snoring. And I thought hitting you with a rock would be cruel," Artemus quipped.

Rapunzel scoffed as she crawled out of the tent. She stretched and drank some water. They broke camp quickly and each ate a handful of nuts and fruit while they planned their route.

"I think we can make it to the site where the driver was found by midday if we move quickly," Artemus said.

"I agree, maybe even earlier if its qui-." A twig snapped.

"Did you hear that?" he whispered.

She focused on her surroundings: leaves rustled in the faint breeze…birds chirped as they waited for their breakfast…then, there, another snap. The only question: was it man or beast? Finn's reminder to be careful echoed in Rapunzel's head.

Artemus scanned the shadows, his head lifted, tuning into his senses. He lived and breathed the hunt, something she knew was ingrained in him since birth. He picked up a small rock and tossed it in the direction of the snapping twig. Stillness. He threw another one, nothing happened.

"Let's split up. I'll go towards him and you just continue on."

"Then?"

"Do you remember the cave marking shown on Alderwick's map?" She nodded. "Good, we'll meet there."

"We don't even know we're in danger, what if it's just a hunter?" she asked.

"Then why haven't they made themselves known, yet?"

"Please be careful." She hated this part, when they had to split up, when they had to put themselves in danger. When they couldn't protect each other.

He dashed across the path the same time she sprinted up and circled through the trees; she could hear Artemus grunting, the sound of a struggle behind her. She paused, debating whether to go back and help him, or keep going. Finn's warning kept running through her mind.

"Watch out," she heard Artemus' shout.

She whipped around, her braids fanning out around her. An arrow thudded into a tree beside her, splintering bark. She dropped to the ground as two more arrows zipped overhead.

Artemus tackled the man, they struggled until he kicked Artemus off him and wrapped his meaty hands around Artemus'

The Journey

neck. He clawed at the man's hands, his eyes bulging.

"The hunter must die," he shouted.

Rapunzel sprang from the ground and lined up her shot. She pulled the string taut, the bow pressed against her chin. The shot connected deep in their assailant's neck; he loosened his grip from Artemus, his hands flying up to the arrow. He fell over clutching the wound, blood flowing between his fingers. His gurgled cries for help were in vain. Artemus, lying next to him panting, checked the man.

"He's gone." Artemus gulped in air, hands rubbed his own neck, before getting up.

"Artemus, are you okay?" Rapunzel asked as she dropped her bow and wrapped her arms around him.

"I'm okay, thanks to you. I just need a moment to catch my breath."

She buried her face in his neck. The earthy scent of his body mixed with the smell of his sweat stirred something within her. Seeing him choked like that, imagining the life disappearing from his eyes…she blinked away tears.

"We can't just stand around here. Are you hurt? Can you get to the cave?" Rapunzel asked.

"I'm fine, but let's check him first."

Rapunzel added his arrows to her quiver, and Artemus took the knife he had in his belt. His satchel had some food and a folded letter inside. She pulled the letter out and opened it, the King's seal was on the top, but the letter was written in neat script.

Follow the traitors. Bring the girl to me.
The hunter must die.

"Morgana?" Rapunzel wondered aloud.

She took a swig of water and passed it to Artemis. He took

four big gulps and handed it back.

"Must be, that's not Alderwick's writing." He took a deep grounding breath and sighed.

She added the letter to her bag. What would Morgana want with her? She must know about the magic her mother left her, and it might be time to tell Artemus what she discovered.

They reached the cave and Rapunzel peered in. The inky blackness stared back. Artemus fumbled with his pack, finally producing a box of matches. A small spark illuminated his face before the fire bloomed. He led the way, his hand clutching his side, using the lit matchstick to guide them.

A few steps in they found an abandoned lantern with unused oil still in the bottom. Artemus lit the lantern, and the soft glow illuminated the cave.

"Are you sure you're not badly hurt?" Rapunzel asked.

"I'm sure, but I should get hurt more often if you'll dote on me like this," he joked.

She ignored his sly comment and inspected the skin on his neck. It was red and would likely bruise. She stepped back, eyes squinted, inspecting every inch of him.

"Take off your shirt, there's blood," she demanded.

He pulled it off, the scratch on his abdomen red and bloody. She pulled out some alcohol and cotton and cleaned the wound. He flinched despite her gentle touch.

The flame cast shadows against Artemus' sculpted chest. The smell of him, sage and leather, made her head buzz. She took a bandage and wrapped it around his abdomen, her fingers traced the contours of his body. His smooth skin rich and dark. He had his eyes closed; his lashes laid gently on his cheeks. Lashes she had always teased him about.

She looked down, remembering her mother singing the song

when she was hurt.

"Hey, are you okay?" His voice rasped, husky in the tight space of the cave.

"Yes." Her cheeks burned red as she stared into his eyes. "I have something to show you." She bit her lower lip to keep it from trembling. She undid one of her braids and placed it in his hand. He hung placed the lantern on the floor beside them. She paused, fear overwhelming her. What if this didn't work, and she was no closer to learning who she was than she was before?

She began to sing, quietly at first, but finding her strength as the familiar words washed over her. The tingle of energy filled the space, and her hair began shimmering. Artemus' mouth hung open; his eyes wide with surprise.

"How did-?" he began, stopping when he saw the long-jagged cut on his side beginning to heal. Rapunzel noticed the red marks around his neck disappearing. She stopped singing and stared into his eyes, the glow of her hair fading.

His free hand reached for her chin and gently tugged her face towards him. Their eyes met and neither of them could break away. He brushed a loose strand of her hair away.

"Your eyes remind me of the forest," he said. "Deep, green, serene with an untamed wildness behind them."

The space between them shrank. Her pulse thundered, a primal drumbeat echoing in her skull. Their lips met in a soft, exploratory kiss. His firm hand delicately cupped her face, deepening their contact.

"Rapunzel," he whispered, sending shivers down her spine when his warm breath fanned over her parted lips.

Without another word, their lips crashed together in an all-consuming kiss that blazed through their bodies like wildfire.

She tasted sweet and wild like honeyed mead, his desire growing with each stroke of her tongue against his.

Her seeking hands roamed down Artemus's chiseled torso, appreciating every ripple of his hard muscles straining beneath her touch. A moan escaped Rapunzel's throat as his palms slipped beneath her tunic, stroking reverently along the tantalizing curve of her hips before finally closing around her full breasts.

"Should I stop?" he asked.

Her chance to end this if she wanted. "No. Don't stop," she whispered.

He continued his exploration of her breasts, gently rubbing his thumb over her pebbled nipples. He lowered his head and took one nipple into his mouth through the fabric; sucking and teasing it with deliberate intent until Rapunzel was squirming with desire.

She unbuckled his waistband, her fingers grazing against the bulge barely contained within his pants. She tugged them down, releasing his throbbing cock.

Touching him was like a lightning bolt of raw arousal; hard flesh hot against her palm as she began to stroke him from base to the swollen tip. His head fell back in ecstasy, each stroke amplified by her firm grip.

Her other hand moved to her own pants, unlacing them. He pushed her hands away with one of his and finished undoing them. They stopped long enough for him to lay her on his outstretched coat. He slid her pants down before removing his own.

He laid next to Rapunzel. His hands stroking the soft skin of her abdomen, his fingers trailing up to her breasts again, his thumbs teasing her. The wetness between her legs was building. He ran his fingers along her inner thighs, coaxing her to open for him. She moaned, hips bucking instinctively against Artemus' hand. His teasing touch made her ache with need.

He positioned himself on top of her. His erection rubbing against her wetness. He slowly entered her, both moaning. Their hips met in a feverish rhythm, their bodies moving as one as they sought relief from the burning lust that consumed them. Artemus groaned against Rapunzel's neck, his teeth grazing softly on the skin there as he pushed deeper into her with each thrust. She ran her fingers through his untamed locs, raking her fingernails along the muscles of his back.

Ecstasy.

Artemus groaned and pressed his thumb against Rapunzel's clit, her orgasm building inside her. He thrust deeper as her cries grew more hurried. They finished within seconds of each other. He kissed her one more time before he rolled off her body and on to his back next to her.

"Do you regret that?" he asked.

"No, why would I? " She replied. "It's no different than any of the other trips we go on, right? Casual fun between friends."

"Last night you didn't seem to want this anymore," he replied.

"I was drunk. I don't even remember what I said."

She put her pants back on, her back to him.

"If you don't want to do this anymore, we don't have to. I respect that."

Rapunzel didn't reply, only gathered her belongings and poked her head outside the cave. The forest was still. Squirrels and rabbits scurried around, a deer grazing in the clearing didn't even bother to lift its head in her direction. No one was looking for them, at least not now.

Rapunzel couldn't stand this tension between them, all these emotions bubbling to the surface ruining their arrangement. Artemus hummed and whistled beside her, unfazed by… everything. That's why it would never work - except it has been for years.

They stopped to rest as the sun was beginning to set. This was Rapunzel's favorite time to be in the forest. When the skies start to turn purple and the sun streams through the trees. Her hair shimmered in the sun.

"I thought you couldn't control it? How did you heal me?"

"I still am not sure, but it has to do with the song. Mama used to sing to me, but the words were written in the journal." She took the journal from her bag, opened it to the page with the incantation, and handed it to him.

He read silently, his eyes scanning the page twice. "Was there anything about my father?"

"I didn't get too far past that but I'm sure there is. Do you want to read it?"

His fingers floated over the edge of the page, his finger twitched slightly. He shut the journal and tossed it to Rapunzel. "I think I'm okay right now." His eyes were downcast, a slight frown crinkling his chin.They spent too much time avoiding the past, now look at them. Her hair glows when she sings and he can't even read his father's name. Rapunzel sighed.

"We should move on before it gets too dark." He stood up, gathered his belongings, and stormed off silently before Rapunzel was even off the ground.

She jogged to catch up and they walked side by side for a bit, the forest was in its quiet phase before the night creatures began to wake up.

'What else can it do? Other than heal. Thank you for that,

The Journey

by the way." Artemus didn't sulk for long, his emotions stayed locked up in his head. When he was ready to move on he just started talking again.

"You're welcome, and I don't know…" She huffed softly "but I think we should read the journal together." His shoulders tensed, his pace quickened. "Just so we can know what this protector thing is all about!"

She rushed to catch up. "Can you slow down and just talk to me!"

He stopped, took a deep breath, and turned slowly. "I don't need to know because this is a one time deal."

"What do you mean?"

"I told you I wanted to leave after this." His voice was void of emotion, but Rapunzel knew something was simmering under the surface. She felt the energy of it sizzling between them.

"You said if." She shook her head, he was being ridiculous talking this way.

Artemus shrugged. " 'If' is quickly becoming yes." He whipped back around and kept walking, leaving Rapunzel mouth open. Shocked, but not surprised. She did it, the one thing she wanted to avoid, she lost him. "You'll need to move faster if you don't want to camp tonight."

Before Rapunzel could process what just happened, they almost missed the turn for the Darkspire Manor, the wooden post covered with overgrown bushes.

"How are we doing this?" Rapunzel asked. "We can't just ask to see the prince."

His stealth and instinct for survival ran through his blood, according to his stories. Rapunzel knew if he read the journal he'd know more. She wanted to, but she didn't want to betray his trust, on top of everything else.

"The path is narrow, we'll walk on either side, watching for any traps, guards, the usual."

Rapunzel was surprised that there weren't more guards, but it was possible Alderwick was wrong and it really was abandoned.

The iron gate threaded with overgrown vines came into view, they noticed one guard leaning against the gatehouse wall, boredom was etched into his ordinary features, his sword beside him. Was he alone?

"Can you hit him with an arrow?" Rapunzel asked.

"Easily, but do we really want to just want to shoot everyone we see?"

"Good point."

"I can sneak up on him, with the sleeping potion. You go around the back and see if there are any others."

"Alright. Be careful."

"You as well." His eyes met hers for a moment, a flicker of emotion in their depths, then he melted into the shadows.

Rapunzel followed the woods around the back of the manor. There was a large tree with a branch that extended closer to the wall. She climbed up the tree, clinging to its branches as she ascended. The thick, sturdy branch she settled on was eye level with the large balcony. She sat and waited for Artemus, not wanting to jump directly into a guard's arms.

Rapunzel huffed in surprise when she saw Prince Leander pacing back and forth on the stone balcony. As if he is on holiday, and not being held against his will. She thought about Artemus' concerns of this being a trap, but why would the prince be here?

She watched him run his hands though his curly blonde hair. His bare chest rose and fell with ragged breaths. She was enamored by the hard lines of his face, familiar and strange

The Journey

all at once. Heat flooded her cheeks. She hadn't seen Leander in ten years, he was much different than the tall, scrawny, boy she gave herself too.

This was a man, a prince too busy to stay in one place. Like herself and Artemus. Was he running from something too?

She shook her head, trying to focus on the situation, on the danger potentially lurking, but her eyes drifted back to him, to their history. She closed her eyes, and Artemus flashed in her mind. His calloused hands on her soft skin and his lips claiming hers in the darkness. She shuddered, heat pooling in her belly.

Leander clasped his hands above his head, staring out into the darkness. Staring right through her. Her fingers curled around the tree branch beneath her, knuckles whitening. She couldn't tear her eyes away from him.

"Zel," Artemus whispered from below.

"Is the coast clear," she called, after composing her thoughts.

He gave her a thumbs up and she loosened one of her braids, looped the strands around the branch, and jumped off. Her hair whipped around her as she slid down its length, the familiar, silky strands wrapping around her body like an old friend. She only learned about its magic yesterday, but she had been taking advantage of it strength since it started to grow. Better than any rope.

Her feet landed on the ground with a soft thud. She took a few moments to braid the loose strands before looking to Artemus for information.

"The guard won't be waking for some time," he said. "I've bound and gagged him, but we should hurry in case he's discovered."

"Any others? What's it look like?"

"I haven't seen or heard any other guards." He pursed his lips, thinking. "Everything is overgrown, this place is abandoned. Did you see anything?"

"Yes, Leander is in that room right there," she said, pointing to the large balcony.

"Then let's find a way in."

Prince Found

"You'd think there'd be more guards," Artemus whispered.

"I know. It's strange. Magic, maybe?" He gave a noncommittal shrug. "If I didn't see the prince for myself, I wouldn't even believe he was here."

The once manicured land of the front lawn was overgrown with wild flowers, weeds, and tall grass. The ivy along the stone walls grew wild, covering almost every inch. It reminded Rapunzel of the Evil Queen who trapped the Princess' tower in thorny rose bushes so no one would find her.

The door to to enter through the kitchen was unlocked. Artemus entered first, listening for any noises but none came. "Really confident no one would come looking?"

"Who would look, if not Morgana?"

The tables were covered in bowls and utensils, whatever food was left behind long gone. The fireplace and ovens were three times as big as those in any tavern she had ever seen.

"Did that book say anything about this place?" Artemus asked.

"There was a bit of information. It belonged to Morgana's elder cousin, no family of her own. After she was buried, the servants just…left"

"Hmm…," He ran his finger over the dust-coated table in the hall. "Clearly leaving everything behind."

Everything in the manor was preserved in time, the stone and timber walls protection from the elements. The large dining table in the center seemed an odd choice for a woman who lived alone. The walls were lined with scenic paintings of the forest around them, and portraits of Darkspires long gone.

"Look." Rapunzel pointed to the large portrait

Above the stone fireplace with snakes carved into its mantle, a portrait of a woman hung. She looked like Morgana, with her angular face, and large almond shaped eyes. This woman was older than her though, her gray wavy hair pulled back in the painting.

Artemus' eyebrows raised when he saw the portrait. "Strong resemblance, huh?"

"No kidding. Shows how much her servants loved her they didn't even take it with them when they left after her funeral."

Rapunzel saw the lift of his cheek, and Rapunzel sighed, he was warming up again. He had to be if he was almost smiling at her bad jokes.

They crept up the steps. The place seemed quiet but they didn't want to be caught off-guard. There was no signs of a struggle, although there were some dirty footprints on the stairs.

The second floor was nothing more than a wood paneled hallway, dotted with paintings, leading to the solarium. The wood floor creaked beneath them as they approached the door. Her heart was hammering in her chest. She was sure the sound of it was echoing around them. Artemus looked calm as ever.

Rapunzel jiggled the handle - locked. She leaned in close to the keyhole, but couldn't see or hear anything.

"He's in here." She tapped her knuckles against the door rapidly. There was no sound on the other side. "Can you pick it?"

Artemus crouched to take his lock picks out of his bag. He was mid attempt when the door swung open in front of them. Leander stood in the doorway, a black tunic hanging over his muscular frame, black leather pants hugging his body.

Leander stared at them; his eyes wide. "Rapunzel? Artemus? What are you doing here?"

"We were sent to find you," Rapunzel said. This was confusing, he didn't look like he needed saving.

"By who?"

"Alderwick." Artemus' eyebrows knitted in confusion, as he stood up.

"Who sent him?" He was taller than Rapunzel remembered, at least by six inches. His green eyes flecked with specks of gold glinted with suspicion.

"He gave us his journal. He was worried you had been kidnapped."

He hesitated but then waved us into the room. The private sitting room was no less opulent than the hall was. Emerald brocade lined the walls, with gold lanterns. There were no portraits in here, but various paintings of more forest scenes lined the walls. It felt like sitting in the middle of the forest.

Leander paced the room, running his hands though his hair, not excited to be found at all. Why was he not more grateful?

"Where is Oliver, my guard?"

"He's fine, taking a little nap," Artemus said. "Why all the questions?"

"You did want to be found, didn't you?" Rapunzel asked. It seemed a ridiculous question, but he hesitated before responding.

"I don't know who I can trust," he said. Rapunzel and Artemus shared a concerned look. "I was attacked in the woods, on my way to the palace. They killed Jack, my guard. Oliver and I were able to hold him off, he was injured badly. We left him for dead and came here to hide in case there were others."

"Who do you think sent them?" Rapunzel asked, wondering what he knew.

"The only person who knew my plans was Morgana." He locked eyes with Rapunzel.

"Why would you come to her family manor to hide?" Artemus stared at him unbelieving. Rapunzel was wondering the same thing, *if you think Morgana is involved why come to her family home?*

"She doesn't know I found it, it was a happy accident many years ago. If it weren't for that portrait in the hall I wouldn't have even realized who it belonged to."

Rapunzel sat on the wooden bench. "We were attacked in the woods." She wondered if Morgana even knew the prince was still alive. *She must have if she sent someone after us.*

Leander stopped pacing and looked at them across the room. "By who?"

"We don't know but the letter had the royal seal on it," Artemus said, his jaw tight. "He had orders to kill me and take Rapunzel. Zel shot an arrow through his neck." *Was he making sure Leander knew they could handle themselves?* Rapunzel didn't think Leander was a threat to them.

"You said Alderwick gave you a journal?" Rapunzel nodded.

Prince Found

"Anything helpful in it?"

"Alderwick suspected that Morgana poisoned your father. Did you know about the Darkspire family and their desire to claim Avalonia?" He shook his head.

"I don't think they expected Morgana, your father might not have been aware himself. But my mother, Theron, and Alderwick were all the protectors of the crown." He fell onto the seat behind him. His head in his hands. Rapunzel continued.

"When she kicked them out of the palace, after she married your father, he was left vulnerable to her attacks. Alderwick alone couldn't protect him. He only prolonged the inevitable."

"I tried to tell my father ages ago. He wouldn't listen. He was smitten with her from the start." He looked up at Rapunzel and Artemus. "How do the two of you play into this?"

"My mother gave me her magic on her death bed. Artemus has his father's enchanted arrows and bow. Alderwick asked for our help."

Leander looked between them. "Thank you both. I never would have expected this." He crossed the room and grasped Rapunzel's hands. "And you, Zellie. After all these years, still courageous."

She hadn't heard that name in years. The sweet memory of stolen childhood kisses in dark corners while he whispered it into her ear flooded her memory. She glanced at Artemus, who was staring daggers at Leander. Her hands dropped to her sides.

"I just wanted to do my part for the kingdom," she said, not wanting to dwell on all the emotions being dredged up. "Do you think it's safe for us to stay here tonight? Or should we make camp in the forest?"

"No!" Artemus said. "Someone else could be headed here. We

should definitely camp out in the forest, away from here. We can manage in the dark, we have before." He stared at Leander, his eyes dark his lips pressed in a firm line. "Is there anything work taking from here?"

"We can take a look. The master bedroom is on the other side and the only room I haven't checked."

Artemis put on his black vest and leather riding coat. He was dressed in the traditional mourning clothes, traveling in anticipation of a funeral. The coat hugged his back and shoulders and Rapunzel couldn't help staring. He slung his sword over his shoulder and turned to face them. He noticed Rapunzel staring and raised his eyebrow. She blushed, shook her head, and looked down all in the same moment before rushing out the door.

The master bedroom was simple compared to the rest of the manor. There was a bookshelf that lined the wall behind the simple canopy bed. The shelves were mostly bare except for a few leftover books and broken trinkets. Artemus walked over to see if there was anything work keeping.

The armoire was a simple wood design, the gold pull knobs the only show of extravagance in the entire room. Resting on top of the dusty piece of furniture was a bell jar. Rapunzel walked towards it, inside was a shriveled water lily completely brown and distorted by time. She lifted the glass to look closer, remembering the title of the page: *Water Lily: The Magic Within*.

She touched the top of it with her finger and a jolt of electricity pulsed through her hand, she pulled back instinctively. She took deep breath and pressed her fingertip to the petal again, this time she resisted the urge to snap her hand back. The tip of the petal began glow and turn pink. Rapunzel gasped. When she pulled her hand away the petal shriveled up once again. She had no idea what it meant but she was taking it with her, maybe Alderwick could help her.

Artemus put a couple of books in his bag and walked over to her. The flower was tucked neatly into her linen handkerchief in her bag.

"Anything good?" he asked. She didn't want to tell him about the flower in front of Leander, not yet anyway.

"Nope, whomever was left behind really picked the place clean."

The trio left the manor. Rapunzel feeling like she had more questions than ever mounting within her.

They made their way back through the forest, Leander wanting to stop at the site of his attack. "Maybe they left behind something we can use." There wasn't, but he stared at the dried blood on the tree: the spot where his driver's body was discovered.

"He died; protecting me," Leander whispered. He bowed his head, his lips trembling in silent prayer.

Rapunzel stood next to him; hands clasped. Her own prayer for safety and clarity running through her head. When he opened his eyes, fierce determination flashed in their depths.

"I will stop her," he said, clenching his fists against his side.

They trekked through the dark forest, Artemus' lantern the only thing lighting the way. Rapunzel's tired brain couldn't even keep track of what they were doing.

"Can we please stop? I can barely keep my eyes open."

Leander yawned loudly behind her. "I could use some sleep."

They lit a small fire for warmth, shared what remained of Martha's food, and laid out under cover of the trees, not having the energy to set up a tent. Within moments, Artemus' gentle snoring filled the space. Rapunzel stared at the sky, unable to sleep. Her mind raced with thoughts of the day's events: discovering she could control her magic, being chased in the woods, the cave, Artemus' reaction, and the feelings seeing Leander had raised. She tossed and turned for a few moments and sighed loudly.

"Zellie, are you awake?" Leander whispered.

Rapunzel considered pretending she was sleeping, but he clearly heard her.

"Yes."

"Thank you, again. For helping me, especially when I've been a terrible friend."

Rapunzel didn't know what to say. She hadn't considered that he even thought of her, of their relationship. What if her mother hadn't died and she remained in the palace day in and day out? What if Morgana hadn't come and put a wedge between the king and his advisors? Would Rapunzel have had a different life, a life with Leander? Would it have been better?

"Well, I guess it goes two ways." She wasn't sure why she downplayed his actions. He was the prince, he could move freely and did, and never sought her or Artemus out.

"I shouldn't have let Morgana's influence over my father get in the way of what we had."

"We were young. We don't even know it would have lasted." Her head swam with confusion. She'd been prepared to hate him when she saw him. The pompous prince who didn't need anyone, but he was still the same person underneath.

"I still feel the same way I did. Do you remember what I said?"

Rapunzel swallowed hard and whispered. "I will make you my Queen one day, Zellie. I promise." At sixteen years old, having been around the palace and its luxuries for a decade, his promise had been everything to her. Her own fairytale.

"Yes. I thought about you, often. And seeing you today, I still want you to be my queen."

She rolled onto her side to face him, he'd already been facing her. He smiled the same cheeky grin he had when he was seventeen.

"Leander, I'm sorry if I am having trouble believing that. You knew where to find me and never bothered." She bit her lower lip to stop from crying. "I admit, being around you- a lot of memories are returning."

"All of them good, I hope."

"No. They haven't all been good. You broke my heart." A tear trickled down her cheek, dripping off her chin onto her blanket. "But it doesn't matter, I can't be Queen. I'm selfish."

"That's not true."

"You don't know me anymore, Leander. I mean I'm only here because Alderwick promised he'd help me control this power. Artemus is tired of my shit too."

"The two of you have stayed friends this whole time?"

She nodded. "We seem to be at odds right now though. Maybe forever, he's going off on his own when this is over."

"You don't want that?"

She wasn't sure why she was telling him all this. Maybe it was the dark, the low whispers, the secrecy of it.

"I don't want to lose him. I don't want anything to change."

Leander nodded, his full lips pursed softly. "Everything changes, Zellie. But I will take your reluctance to mean I can still win you over." He winked playfully and Rapunzel smiled despite her warring emotions.

He extended is hand toward her and she reached back. His smooth palms were a sharp contrast to Artemus' calloused hands. She couldn't stop herself from imagining Leander's hands tracing the curve of her hips, showing her how much he missed her all these years. Then her thoughts flitted to Artemus again. His constant presence in her life and her unwillingness to see if that could bloom into something more. She rolled onto her back, pulling her hand from his, waiting for sleep to push the thoughts away.

Rapunzel was the first to rise the next morning, She'd packed up camp by the time Artemus and Leander were wiping the sleep from their eyes.

"Are we ready?" Rapunzel asked, when they men had rolled up their blankets.

"Let's go," Artemus said; coolly. He had refused to make eye contact with.

She didn't want to ask him what was wrong with Leander there, because she was certain it had to do with him. When Leander wandered into the woods alone, she pulled Artemus aside.

"I have something to show you, I found a dead flower in the bedroom, it did something weird when I touched it."

"Now you want to share secrets with me?" he asked. Rapunzel knitted her brow, unsure what he even meant.

"Are you okay? I know it's been a tough couple of days."

"I'm just ready to keep moving and be done with this whole mess."

Rapunzel left him to stew by himself. He clearly was dealing with his own issues, and didn't want to open up to her. She took a deep breathe. She wasn't being fair, it was her reluctance to talk to him that started this all to begin with.

The conversation between the three of them on the walk was nothing more than idle small talk about their travels. Rapunzel not wanting to look like she was favoring either man, kept all her remarks short and to the point. Alderwick's cottage was made entirely of wood with blue paint trimming the windows. It was tucked away at the edge of the forest, close to the palace so he could easily travel back and forth.

They approached the cottage and noticed a pair of boots sticking out of the bushes. They were attached to one of the palace guards; long claw marks were burrowed into his chest. Artemus checked his pulse. "He's long gone."

He scanned the area and pointed to another set of bushes. "Check over there."

Leander walked to the bush and crouched down. "Another guard, this one has two arrows in his back and the same claw marks on his neck." He walked back towards them.

"Should he check inside?"

They both nodded and Artemus led us into the hushed interior. The disarray of parchment and instruments seemed untouched, but Rapunzel couldn't be sure. However, the small table and chairs were knocked over, along with a lantern. It's oil spilt on the floor.

"Over there," Artemus pointed.

The soft tapping of boots on the wooden floorboards echoed. The bundle in the corner began to writhe. Artemus approached slowly his shoulders tensed. He crouched down, then visibly relaxed.

"It's Finn," he said, beginning to untie him.

Leander rushed forward to kneel by Finn's side, removing the gag. His eyes grew wide at the sight of the missing prince. "Prince Leander, you're alive!"

"Who did this?" Leander asked.

Finn coughed, taking in deep gulps of air as Artemus removed the rope around his wrists.

Forbidden Love

"Thank you," he rasped.

"Who did this to you?" Rapunzel asked again.

"Guards… They were asking for the journal. They took him—"

"Alderwick? When did it happen?" Leander's tone was urgent, his hands still supporting Finn's shoulders.

"The night after we were in Oakwood." The night before they were attacked.

"Did you hear anything else? After they left with Alderwick. A beast? A fight?" Rapunzel asked.

"Why?" Finn replied, his brow creased, eyes squinted.

"There are two guards slumped in the bushes." Artemus stood and helped Finn up. "Claw marks and one had three arrows in his back."

"No, but Alderwick can shape shift, but I don't think he would have killed them. I might know where he's hiding though."

"Where?" Artemus asked.

"In the forest, hidden by magic. I'll lead you there."

Finn picked up his lute and led them out into the forest once again. The sun shone overhead, they heard the distant chopping of wood and chatter of woodcutters. They filled Finn in on what had happened the last two days, he listened attentively.

He slowed down and began looking at the trees more closely. "That's the one." He turned right and when Rapunzel looked at the tree, she noticed the same symbol from the from to this journal etched in the tree. The took was overgrown with tree roots and dead branches and leaves.

"Are you sure this is the right way?" Leander asked.

"Trust me," Finn responded. "I have my ways of finding what's hidden."

He began strumming his lute softly, the melody of her

mother's song wafting through the trees. Rapunzel could feel the tingle of magic on her skin as they journeyed deeper into the trees, but without the words, her hair remained dormant. An unnatural chill filled the air warning them away, but the louder the lute became the more Rapunzel could feel Alderwick's pull. The loose strands of her hair vibrated. A hut materialized before them.

"He's inside." He reached for the handle and twisted it. The wooden door creaked open.

Alderwick lay on the floor; pale and unmoving. "Alderwick!" Rapunzel rushed in first. His eyes fluttered open at the sound of her voice. "You've come." His voice was weak, ragged.

"What happened?"

"The guards were sent for me," he grimaced. "But when we left, we were attacked by a hunter and he had a wolf with him. Magical, I think. He got my arm before I was able to shift into a bird and fly away."

"The guards were killed," Rapunzel explained.

"We were attacked at our camp the next morning," Artemus said. "Rapunzel killed him when he tried to choke me."

Alderwick sighed and struggled to sit up. His gaze settled on Leander. A grin stretched across his face.

"Prince Leander, they found you."

"Yes, but I wasn't kidnapped. I was attacked but got away. My guard and I hid out Darkspire Manor, but I sent him back to my home."

Alderwick nodded. "Since the beginning I knew something was off about her, but I could never prove anything. I had to rely on people I trusted and over the years, those numbers have dwindled to a handful." He winced, the deep scratches on his arm inflamed.

"Will my magic work on you?" Rapunzel asked.

His eyes widened. "You figured it out?" She nodded.

"I think if Finn plays his lute, it will strengthen its power."

Finn began strumming the melody on his lute once more. Artemus watched from the other side of the hut. Rapunzel undid her braid again and wrapped it around Alderwick's hand. She could feel the energy building within her, she began to sing the incantation, her hair glowing like the sun.

"How is this happening?" Leander asked Artemus.

"Watch."

As she reached the end of the verse, Alderwick's eyes lost their listless look. He sat up on his own strength . She finished the song and braided her hair. Finn played one more verse on his lute before silence filled the hut.

"Thank you," Alderwick said, his eyes glinting with excitement. "I knew you would figure it out."

"I recognized the words in the journal and started singing," she explained. "I remembered she used to sing it when I was hurt, I tested it on Artemus and it worked."

Leander drew her into his arms, enveloping her in the scent of pine trees. "That was amazing."

"Thank you," she pulled away, eager to focus on the task ahead. "Alderwick, I found something in the manor I want to show you." She unwrapped the wilted water lily and laid it on the table in the center of the sparse hut. The rest of them huddled around the table. "It was under a glass dome in the master bedroom, but look…"

She touched the tip of the flower again and the same thing happened. The spark of gold before the color began to return. It bloomed back to life, its delicate scent filling the air as its petals opened. Rapunzel removed her finger and it once again wilted.

"Solaria told me about this. The last one was stolen but it lives on in your bloodline. That's why she had to pass her magic to you, or it would have died with her.

"Why would the flower have died this way though? If its magic wouldn't it stay alive?"

"Do you still have the journal?" he asked. Rapunzel took it out of her bag and handed it to him.

He flipped through the pages until he found what he was looking for. He turned it to Rapunzel, the story of the flower. It can turn back the clock for one full life if taken right at the moment of death. If its used sparingly, the magic will live on forever. A vision of the portrait in the grand hall came to mind.

"Artemus, the portrait in the manor," Rapunzel turned to him, his eyes flashed in recognition and he sat straight up.

"It looked exactly like Morgana, with white hair. The resemblance like it was her own mother."

"It was eerie," Leander added.

Rapunzel's eye widened, she rummaged through her bag and pulled out the letter they found on their attacker. She showed it to Alderwick. "She wants me. Is it because of the magic?"

"I don't know for sure. It's possible, if her magic is fading, she'd be looking for the source to gain strength."

"I think I know what needs to be done though." Alderwick locked eyes with Rapunzel, his brow creased, his lips a thin line. "It will take a sacrifice from you Rapunzel."

"What do you mean? Will I have to die?" The thought hadn't occurred to her.

"No, but you might have to sacrifice your magic," Rapunzel straightened her back and stepped away from the table. How dare he even suggest that? Give away the last piece of her mother.

"I don't think I can do that."

"If I could find way to avoid it I will, but we need to head back to the workshop. You can rest there while I work."

They left the hut and walked back through the forest. As they entered the woods the hut disappeared into the unknown.

Artemus tugged Rapunzel's braid to get her attention. He waved her closer and stopped them, until the rest were out of earshot. They began walking at a much slower pace.

"Are you really considering this?" His head was turned in her direction, his eyes laced with concern. He tucked in his cheek in the thoughtful way he did when he was mentoring someone.

"No, not unless he can figure out another way. If he can't I'm done with this."

"Are you sure? Didn't sound that way last night?" his voice had a hard edge to it. Rapunzel wasn't sure what he meant.

"What do you mean?" Did he hear their late night conversation? She thought about what she told Leander about Artemus. Did it come off as cold and uncaring from his point of view? Was it cold and uncaring?

"The two of you, whispering in the dark, I heard what he said. That he'll win you over. Your reluctance."

Rapunzel stopped and turned to him. "You heard the last part of a conversation that included me telling him he broke my heart. That doesn't mean I'd take him back now."

"But you didn't tell him no," he looked down, a dead bird laying it his feet. "My grandfather used to say dead birds meant change was coming. I guess this is my sign."

For the second time in as many days, Artemus left Rapunzel standing, mouth opened, as he stormed off. It wasn't a coincidence. Two dead birds at our feet, change was inevitable.

Behind the Palace Walls

They arrived at the workshop and helped Alderwick straighten up. Nothing was taken, they just wanted his journal, which thankfully Rapunzel and Artemus had. While they ate a meal of nuts, bread, fruit, and wine; Alderwick began scouring his books of magical plants for any information. While they freshened up and laid down to rest; he practiced spells that would help him preserve Rapunzel's magic. By the time they woke the next morning, Alderwick had a plan that would rid them of Morgana and allow Rapunzel to retain her magic.

"First, let me say thank you for even being willing to take this on. I understand it is not something you were prepared for."

Rapunzel still wasn't sure if she was willing but she would at least hear him out. "Listening takes no effort."

"The arrows from Theron, they are enchanted to destroy

magical creatures, but Solaria, and now Rapunzel's magic were exempt, being one of the protectors. It's a plan passed down to each generation of protectors. I wonder if all along we've been fighting the same evil."

"What sacrifice do I have to give?"

"In order for the arrow to work, the magic that she took from that flower needs to be drained from her. If you died that would be one way, but we can avoid that but using the flower you found."

Artemus stared at Rapunzel, shaking his head. "Zel, you can't do this. That's who you are!"

Her eyes were closed. She heard her mother's last words: *My gift to you.*

"There's no way I can keep my magic?" She didn't care if it sounded selfish. Even if she never used it again, it was all she had left of her mother. All she had left of the past at this point.

"There's a very small window, if Artemis can shoot accurately, the moment when your power leaves you, you may be able to take it back again, like you did in the hut."

She looked around the room, at all these people who were willing to help but only she had to give everything up. Nothing about this seemed fair.

"Artemus, can you do it?"

"I'm sure I can, but what if I don't? What if I miss? What then?"

"I trust you." They locked eyes, another flicker of emotion in the deep blue of his. She knew those three words couldn't fix everything between them, but he nodded.

"Thank you." Leander said, reaching for her hand. She wouldn't pretend this was going to be easy for her. She wouldn't coddle anyone's feelings by accepting their fake praise either. She would do what she had to do and be rid of all of this. Everyone could go their own way, Artemus included. He pulled his hand back.

"Let's just go."

They began walking towards the palace, each contemplating their role in the plan ahead.

"We can't just stroll in there," Artemus huffed, with his hands firmly on his hips, as the palace walls came into view. Rapunzel could sense his frustration rising, but she didn't know how to ease it. She didn't even know how to ease her own.

"You're right," she agreed. "The guards might be looking for Leander already, for all of us."

Artemus looked in their direction, glossing over Rapunzel. "Any ideas, Leander? It is your palace."

"There's a secret passage, in the fields, by the well," Leander said, his gaze already locked in the direction they would need to go. "It'll bring us to the cellar under the main kitchen."

"Won't there be people in the kitchen?" Rapunzel asked.

"I can distract them," Finn said. "They're used to seeing me around."

"Good idea," Leander replied. "This way."

The well was in an isolated area, closer to the farmland that provided crops for the palace. The fields were empty due to the mandatory mourning period in the Kingdom. They didn't have to worry about being noticed.

"Here," Finn revealed a trap door hidden beneath dirt and leaves. "What about the lock?"

"I got it," Artemus said, pulling out his picks. The familiar click was music to their ears.

Artemus lifted the iron door and stepped aside allowing Leander and Finn to lead the way.

"Wait," Artemus said, grabbing her elbow.

She swallowed hard and turned around to face him. She had hoped for a chance to talk to him alone, but right now her mind was preoccupied with breaking into the palace. She raised her eyebrow. "Yes."

"We can walk away from this now. Nothing would change for us if we just left." His face was determined.

"I can't do that. I can't leave Avalonia forever. Why can't you understand that!" she cried, tears filling her eyes.

"You can, Zel. You do it all the time, but why do we come back? Life changes, I wish you would realize that before you waste yours trying to recapture what was."

She dropped her head to hide the tears that slipped past her lashes.

"Everything okay?" they heard Leander call from the open hatch.

"We should go. They're waiting on us," she said, her voice husky with tears. Rapunzel bit her lip, mulling over his words, over what Leander said. Why did this have to be complicated? Why did Leander dredge up so many memories for her?

"You don't want to be with me. At least not for more than a fun night every now and then."

Rapunzel didn't know how to respond to that. She didn't even really think of love – not until it seemed like she had to make a choice. She pursed her lips and took a deep breath.

"I'm sorry you feel that way, Artemus." She climbed down the tunnel, always escaping reality. Would she ever learn that never solves her problems?

"Stay close," Leander said, his voice echoing off the damp walls.

The four of them skulked through the dark underground passage. The smell of dirt and decay filled their senses. Each footstep amplified in the narrow space.

"Do you smell that?" Artemus whispered, his hunter's senses kicking into high gear.

Just then, a menacing growl cut through the tunnel. A massive black wolf emerged, its eyes gleaming yellow in the dark. Rapunzel grabbed one the daggers she carried. "Get down!" she screamed, the blade flying from her hand with ease. She struck its sinewy neck, its howl echoing in the confined space.

"Behind me!" Leander roared, unsheathing his sword. He stood as a shield between them and the snarling wolf. Their deadly exchange was a frantic blur of his sword connecting with claws, flesh, and teeth.

"Don't move," Artemus whispered, so close she could feel his breath on her neck.

An arrow ripped past Rapunzel's head and the loud wet noise of the arrow puncturing its eye, then a faint silver glow. The enchanted arrows. The wolf howled once, the metallic smell of blood in the air. Leander took advantage of its confusion and lifted his silver sword. The blade cut through the dark with a swish and the beast's head rolled away from its body.

"We must be almost there," Leander said.

They reached another ladder and Leander ascended first, followed by Finn. Before Rapunzel could head upwards towards the light, Artemus stopped her.

"Must be nice to have two men to keep you alive now," he said, the weak light from the exit casting dark shadows on his angular face.

She wanted to grab him, kiss him, make him see how much she cared for him. But instead she gripped the rung with both hands, her body shaking. His words were devoid of any emotion, devoid of the friendship and love they had for each other. She sensed him behind her, his steady breathing familiar to her. They had gone so long without any issues, their arrangement working fine.

She didn't even consider Leander in that way, not really. It was the memories that made her weak; not him. But the memories that felt as real to her as the memories of her mother. What was right?

Leander reached for her hand and helped her up when she reached the top. A smile on his face before he pressed his lips to her hand. His warm full lips on her knuckles sent jolts up and down her arm. She pulled away, needing to stay focused on survival. One thing was for sure, she needed to figure out what she wanted before the decision was made for her.

The cellar was familiar to them. Rapunzel, Leander, and Artemus used to play hide and seek down there. The shelves stocked with mead, wine, and food was their playground. When they were teenagers, it became the place she and Leander would sneak off to kiss. The memory sent warm waves to her belly.

She clenched her fists, nails biting into her palms, willing the memories away.

They climbed stone steps, pausing at the wooden door that led into the kitchen. Finn poked his head out. He exited and slammed the door shut.

"Good morning, Betty! Could you help…."

"How long should we wait?" Rapunzel whispered.

Leander opened the door, listened for voices, then waved them forward. They walked through the kitchen to the now empty dining room. The walls covered in a rich brocade with lanterns hanging around the room. Portraits of King Magnus, Queen Morgana, and Prince Leander were above the large stone mantle. Leander stopped in front of the portrait of his father, and pounded his fist to his chest, a sign of respect in Avalonia. He closed his eyes, kissed the knuckles on his right hand, and continued forward.

Rapunzel wondered how he was truly coping with the loss of his father in the midst of this craziness. She was beginning to realize how self-centered she had; she had made this entire thing about her and her magic, but this was everyone's life.

The grand corridors were quiet as they crept along, watching and listening for guards. But none came. *Where was everyone?* The period of mourning would normally mean people would be paying their respects to the Queen. Had she isolated everyone so much that no one cared to pay their respects? Or were they turning people away.

The doors to the throne room were ornately embossed gold doors with the royal family's emblem. A tower with a long ivy vine twisting upwards; in the center of the tower a symbol she never really noticed before. *The Protectors.*

Their mission felt destined now. A dance that's repeated over and over again throughout time. Would this be the final act?

Hushed voices drifted from the slightly open doors. Leander motioned for the three of us to hide in a small, covered alcove next to the throne room. Their view was limited from this angle, but Finn kept a lookout.

Rapunzel gasped at the echo of footsteps in the distance.

"He's going to get caught," Finn whispered, as the guards came into view, and he snapped the curtain shut.

"Stop right there!" the guard's voice boomed. "Drop your weapon and kick it towards us."

Leander's sword clattered to the ground. Rapunzel's heart was a battering ram against her chest.

"Phillip, that's the prince," a second guard said. "Won't the queen be thrilled he's returned."

The three of them were silent as statues as they listened to the scene unfold.

"I've come to claim my rightful place as ruler of Avalonia."

"Bold words for a dead prince."

The sound of the guard's sword hitting the stone ground made Rapunzel jump. She could feel Artemus tense next to her. Finn peeked through the gap in the curtain.

"I can't see anything! His sword is still on the floor." Rapunzel's nerves were shot, the clashing of sword against stone and Leander grunts.

"Grab him, Marshall," Phillip said.

"What is happening out here?" Morgana's melodic voice rang out.

"The prince was snooping around outside the doors, your majesty."

"You finally decided to stop being a petulant child and come mourn your father?"

"I was attacked, but somehow I think you know that," Leander replied dryly.

"Do you think you can just walk back in here and make demands?" she asked.

"Take him to the tower. If he's being helped, they'll show their face sooner or later."

The door to the throne room slammed shut. Through the gap in the drape, Rapunzel saw Leander being dragged away by the two guards.

The Tower

"What do we do?" Rapunzel wondered.

"I know where the tower is," Finn said. "But I don't know how walking into her trap is helpful."

"I can get out of the tower through the window."

"Not all of us, if we're trapped. It would take too long." Artemus was right.

"Alright, you get Leander, we'll meet by Alderwick's old study. Leander knows where it is. Let's go, I'll lead you to the tower door."

They raced down winding dimly lit corridors, hiding in dark corners to avoid being seen. They reached the doorway that led up to the tower.

"We'll meet you later, be careful." Finn and Artemus disappeared down the hall. Rapunzel opened the door to the tower and listened. Were the guards gone, did they stay up there with him. She had no way of knowing but she had no time to waste either.

The spiral staircase creaked and groaned under her weight.

The Tower

The sound echoed and she worried that she would be caught. She reached the top and the door creaked open with a squeal.

"Leander," she whispered. "Are you here?"

"Zellie!" She entered the small room, bare except for a small bed and desk. Leander was chained to the wall, the heavy iron clasp around his ankle. "You came, but where are Finn and Artemus?"

His face was lined with thick red welts, where the guards hit him. His left eye was swollen shut and his lips were bloody. Rapunzel rushed to his side, checking his wounds. "How bad does it hurt? I can heal them." She began unbraiding one of the strands, but Leander put his hand over hers.

"Don't. We don't know that won't tip Morgana off. She doesn't know you're here, let's keep it that way for now."

Rapunzel hated knowing she could heal his wounds, but he had a point. Her magic may end up like a beacon, leading Morgana right to her. She looked around the small room and spotted a key hanging on a nail near the door. She tried it in the lock around his ankle. It clicked open.

He removed the shackle and rubbed his ankle; it hadn't been on long enough to do any damage, but his face was miserable. Rapunzel used the remaining water she had and a piece of fabric to clean the wounds as best she could without hurting him. He flinched when she touched his lips.

"I'm sorry," she whispered. He raised his hand to her face and gently stroked his thumbs over her soft skin. He moved closer, her hand dropping between them, he leaned in and brushed his bruised lips over her smooth ones. Rapunzel felt her resolve weakening.

After all the chaos, she just wanted to be held. She wanted to feel cared for. He pulled her closer, and she closed the space between them. Memories of her 16th birthday flooding her. The imprint of his hands on her thighs, his fingers caressing her belly, his lips on her neck. She shivered under his touch.

He captured her lips with his own, kissing her deeply. She moaned, her lips parting under his, her fingers raked through his hair.

"You taste just as sweet as I remember," he murmured. The sound of his voice snapped Rapunzel out of her stupor. This was not what she wanted – at all. She pulled away from Leander.

"Is everything okay?" His eyebrows knitted in confusion.

"We shouldn't do this. I -, It's not right." She straightened her braids and stood up.

"You seemed to be enjoying it. I don't understand." Rapunzel didn't want to lead him on, but she knew her heart did not belong to Leander. His touches weren't familiar to her anymore, not like Artemus'.

"It was very nice, but you aren't –."

"I'm not Artemus," he finished. She shook her head in denial, and he chuckled. "I'm not blind, but it's okay, my broken heart will live another day."

She rolled her eyes and playfully hit his arm. Glad that uncertainty around her feelings for him cleared up. Memories were powerful, but she was done letting them control her life.

Noises in the stairwell plunged them back into reality. Leander opened the door and the guard's voices drifted towards them.

"We're trapped," he said. "She must have planned for this."

"She may have planned for someone to come rescue you, but she didn't plan for me to have a backup plan." She peeked out the tower window and saw they would be able to get down to the outer walkways of the main floor. "Do you trust me?"

The Tower

"Of course, but -"

"We're going out the window. Watch." She undid the length of her braids and with a fluid motion released the golden waves out the window. They spilled down to the ground.

"Wow." Leander's eyes with wide with awe, a smile of appreciation plastered on his face.

"Help me with this."

She grabbed the end of her hair and doubling it over, winding it around the beam that framed the window. It groaned under the added weight.

"Is it strong enough?"

"It's held Artemus and I before. It will hold us now," she promised. The strands as taut as the string of her bow.

He fingered the strands of her hair, assessing it strength, wondering if it would hold his weight.

"Leander," she snapped. "You need to go first. Now!"

"Will you be okay?"

"Yes, I'll be fine. Go!"

He hesitated for a split second before grasping the strands firmly. Rapunzel watched, heart lodged in her throat, as he swung his legs over the sill, the coarse strands wrapped securely around his hands.

"Be careful," she urged.

"Always am," he shot back with a grin that was equal parts bravado and charm. And then, with a deep breath that mirrored, he began his descent.

The persistent tug of her hair made her feel like she had no control of her body. She gripped the support beam until she felt his grip loosen and her body become her own again. She peeked out the window and he waved from below. With trembling hands, she gathered the scattered ends of her courage. Her grip tightened around the locks of hair, finding comfort in its familiar silkiness.

"Here goes nothing," she whispered. The hair slipped through her fingers in controlled increments, gravity tugging her toward the ground. The exhilaration of the flight tingled through her veins every time she had to do this. It was a feeling she never got used to. She landed on the ground and stumbled. Leander steadied her and helped gather her hair into her braids once again.

They sat, back against the stone wall, steadying their breathing. "We need to meet them by Alderwick's old study. They're probably waiting for us."

Leander nodded and grabbed her hand, pulling her through a doorway that would lead us to the main floor.

"The guards probably figured out I've escaped by now. We need to stay alert." Rapunzel and Leander stalked through the palace, hiding in the shadows, avoiding guards.

"How are we going to get to Alderwick's study without being seen?" The guards could be heard in the distance and she worried about Artemus. She knew Finn's presence in the palace wouldn't set off any alarms, so she hoped that would be enough to keep them both safe.

"Alderwick's study is in the opposite side of the throne room." Two guards dashed by them, they backed into the shadows until they were gone. "We need to be fast and keep to the shadows. We can't cross the main hall, so we need to go through the back hallways."

As they moved through the palace, guards were coming in and out of closed doors, shouting to check various rooms and areas of the palace. Rapunzel spotted Finn and Artemus dash from behind a curtain across the hall to a room the guards just

The Tower

came out of.

"Look," Rapunzel pointed, showing Leander where they went.

"Let's go," Leander ran across the hall with Rapunzel behind him. He opened the door slowly.

"Finn…Artemus…are you here?"

Finn popped his head out from behind an end table. "Finally, we found each other."

Artemus joined them from his hiding spot in the closet. "What now? Not exactly easy for four of us to move around undetected."

"The study is around this corner. That area of the palace has been closed off, since Alderwick was forced to work from his cottage." Finn explained, with an air of authority. Rapunzel wondered how long Alderwick had been preparing him for this, but was grateful he had.

"Alright, let's go. Finn, you should lead the way. If any guards see you, just tell them you saw someone sneaking around in the other direction." Finn nodded and the four of them walked into the hallway.

The heavy wooden door of what used to be Alderwick's study was locked. This had to be the end of the road, if they couldn't get into the study they wouldn't be able to defeat Morgana. When Finn produced the key to the door, the one that Alderwick had been holding on to all these years, Rapunzel sighed.

The sweet scent of wood polish filled the air as they entered the study. How strange, Finn had said this area had been closed off. Why would the room be cleaned? Artemus lit one of the lanterns and soft light filled the room. Shelves lined all the walls with books and glass jars filled with liquids, crystals, and herbs.

"I thought this room wasn't used," Rapunzel said.

"Alderwick said it wasn't, but it seems clean and organized, lived in."

Did they stumble upon Morgana's secret? Rapunzel walked over to the large desk in the middle of the room. Books and papers were scattered all over the top along empty vials and crystals.

"Come help me look through these papers."

Artemus and Finn joined her, while Leander inspected the shelves. After a few moments, Artemus snatched a small notebook, not unlike his own, off the table. "Listen to this!"

It worked. He finally is beginning to show symptoms
Of illness. It will be no time at all before I can rule Avalonia.
Centuries of trying, finally at my fingertips.

Centuries. Rapunzel again thought of the portrait in Darkspire Manor. The striking resemblance to Morgana. How strange it was that everyone just up and left and no other family claimed the home.

Leander's face was contorted in anger. His chest rising and falling with each ragged breath. His father's death, and the attack on his life, were because of her. She locked eyes with him, trying to convey that she would fight with him.

"Let's see what else there is, I think there may be more of these journals over on the wall," Finn said.

They each scoured through her old journals, mostly personal affirmations of her greatness, spells she jotted down. She outlined and changed her plan many times over the years, her delusions were endless, but the most delusional people were often successful. She believed she was unstoppable and so she was.

"Hey, Zel," Artemus called. "Come here." Rapunzel walked

The Tower

over to him and he handed her a small red leather journal.

Those fools. Trying to tell him I wasn't fit to be Queen.
  Their last meal will be a slow death for them.

Rapunzel blinked and read it twice more, was she responsible for my mother's death. For Theron's? Was that why she had to give me her magic in secret? More questions than will ever really be answered, but at least now she could enact her revenge.

There were few mentions of her actual powers, but she did talk about having the flower where no one will find it. How surprised she'll be to find out the flower was in Rapunzel's possession.

Wicked Witch

"What else did we need from here, Finn?" Rapunzel asked, wondering why he would tell us to meet here if he thought it was abandoned.

"Oh, I thought Alderwick might have left something that would help us." His eyes darted back and forth between the three of us. Artemus squinted, assessing Finn's sudden change in demeanor. "This was much better though." He ran his fingers through his messy hair, much different than the dapper gentleman he normally presented as.

"You seem so nervous," Leander said. Finn smiled, but it didn't reach his eyes, it was calculated.

The door creaked open behind them, and Morgana walked in. Her black mourning gown hugged her generous curves. Her normally flowing ebony waves, hair very similar to Finn's, is in a severe bun atop her head. Her ruby and diamond crown glittering in the light of her lantern.

"You've done Mommy proud, Finnian." Rapunzel's mouth dropped open, she blinked and shook her head. She couldn't

Wicked Witch

have heard that correctly. Finn was Morgana's son. How could they not know? How could Alderwick not know?

"What did you say?" Leander asked. "He's your son?"

That smile never left Finn's face. "Yes, I am. Nobody figured it out, don't feel so bad. Why do you think my lute and your hair pair so nicely together?"

Rapunzel felt her rage building. He baited them - marched them right into her hands.

"Rapunzel needs to go back up to the tower. Artemus and Leander are unimportant, so I don't care what you do with them." Morgana's red lips spewed malice - the indifference towards their lives clear as day.

"I'm just as powerful as you, even without the lute. If he plays for you, he plays for me - and we'd still be evenly yoked."

Morgana paused and narrowed her eyes. Her lips pursed as she considered what Rapunzel offered. She didn't know Rapunzel wasn't practicing, she only knew what Finn told her.

Rapunzel raised her hands. "I'm willing to give it all up to stop you. Are you willing to do the same?"

While Morgana and Finn were distracted by Rapunzel's attempt to buy time, Artemus, who had been hiding out of sight, nocked an arrow. He shot Finn in the stomach. Morgana screamed and blasted the back of the room. Rapunzel heard Artemus hit the floor. While Morgana tended to Finn, trying to save him, Rapunzel took advantage of the distraction and took the flower out of her bag. She closed her eyes and began singing the song. She didn't care if Artemus would be able to shoot the arrow, she didn't care if she lost her magic, she cared about putting an end to this. If she gave it all up, they could easily kill Morgana enchanted arrow or not.

The incantation poured out of her, stronger than she had ever felt it flow from her. It pulsed in her blood. Morgana could also sense it, she forgot her injured son and turned to Rapunzel. As the flower came back to life; and the magic was pulled from her, Rapunzel locked eyes with Morgana. She had transformed into the woman from the portrait. Power draining from her withered body, she was helpless to fight it.

Rapunzel accepted her fate in that moment and finished the song and the last sliver of magic left her. Leander plunged his sword into the pulsing center of the water lily as Artemis' last enchanted arrow plunged into Morgana's heart. Rapunzel's hair faded to the brown, except for one golden strand that glimmered in the light of the lantern.

Rapunzel ran to Artemis and threw her arms around him. "Thank you." Their lips met in dark corner, and she yearned to continue but he pushed her away gently.

Artemus stood up and the three of them left the study. Leander, without Morgana around to object, ordered the guards to call off their search. While Leander took back control of his kingdom, Rapunzel and Artemus went back to Alderwick's cottage to share the news.

Once Rapunzel and Artemus were alone, outside the palace walls, she collapsed in his arms. The weight of knowing heavier than she ever imagined. He held her and let her cry in his shoulder. Whatever was building between them, slowly starting to crumble once more. Rapunzel had closure and her memories, but no magic. Her hair was still long, but now it felt unnecessarily heavy. They walked back to Alderwick's with the atmosphere of a funeral march. The inevitable change she had tried to avoid coming at her from every direction.

At Alderwick's she lay in bed, listening to their hushed whispers as Artemus recounted the events of the day. She couldn't see them, but she imagined the horror on Alderwick's face as he learned of Finn's betrayal. Did he feel guilty? Did he know Morgana poisoned them? Rapunzel had so many questions but no energy to ask them. She closed her eyes and let sleep come, tomorrow there might be answers.

Endings & Beginnings

The next morning, Rapunzel was greeted by Leander, Alderwick, and Artemus sitting around the table speaking about the palace.

"There she is, thought I was going to have to hit you with that rock after all." Artemus seemed in better spirits today, but we all were. Morgana was gone, her eternal reign had ended.

"I'm glad you're up, please grab something to eat, and join us," Leander said before turning back to the other two.

She filled her plate and joined them at the table. "Good morning, everyone."

Leander cleared his throat, eager to get his big announcement out of the way. "Alderwick agreed to come back and work and live in the palace again."

Rapunzel looked up and smiled. "That's wonderful, Alderwick."

"But," Leander continued. "I was hoping the two of you would come as well."

Rapunzel considered what he said as she chewed and swallowed. Artemus huffed in the background. He would be unimpressed with the offer.

"Doing what? I don't have magic anymore. Artemus used the last arrows his family had to defeat her. We fulfilled our purpose, didn't we?"

"It's not about that. Artemus is still a skilled hunter, of traditional and magical creatures and Alderwick can teach you."

Alderwick nodded. "If even one drop is in you, I can coax it out again. I can also teach you about herbalism, spell casting, everything you'd want to know."

Rapunzel thought of that golden strand, hidden in her dark tresses, no one knew about it but her. If they did, she was sure they'd try to sway her decision.

"I just want you to know the Kingdom - I - appreciate all you have done."Leander said. "Take all the time you need to decide, at the very least you'll have a place to call home."

Rapunzel and Artemus caught each other's eye. She raised an eyebrow in question, his face remained neutral. He was playing his cards close today. "That is a generous offer, thank you." Rapunzel fidgeted in her seat.

Leander shook his head, bewildered look in his eyes, and began to stand. "We are having gathering to remember my father this evening. She buried him without me, I need to honor him."

Rapunzel watched as he said goodbye and walked out of the cottage. Before the conversation could turn back to Leander's offer, she needed to know one thing.

"Alderwick, did you know she poisoned them?"

"I wondered, I suspected, but I had no way to prove it. I had hoped it wasn't true."

Artemus, tipped back in his chair, looked at Rapunzel across the table. "Does knowing make it any less painful?" The eternal debate between them. His not caring and her obsessive need to know.

"No. It doesn't. Does that make you happy?" She stood up and glared at Artemus across the table. "I need to find something to wear for tonight, I suppose. What about you?"

He shook his head. "I'll manage, I have errands to run. I'll see you tonight." \

She nodded and left the table quickly, not trusting herself to keep the emotions threatening to explode from her under the control.

What was meant to be a mournful atmosphere at the palace, ended up being celebratory. Members of the court and other invited guests, toasted to King Magnus' memory and Prince Leander's upcoming coronation over tables overflowing with food. Roasted meats and vegetables, stews, sauces, different types of breads lined the tables and people grazed all evening. The palace servants seamlessly refilled baskets, bowls, platters, and carafes so that no one went hungry or thirsty.

Members of court and nobles from other Kingdom's paid their respects to Leander and couldn't want to meet Rapunzel and Artemus. Artemus avoided the praise by sitting alone with a drink in his hand. His expressionless face and stiff demeanor didn't welcome conversation.

After Rapunzel got tired of making small talk with strangers, she spotted Artemus by the roaring fire in the courtyard. She sat next to him on the stone bench, neither of them speaking for a long moment, just enjoying the warmth of the fire in the dark of night. As they had so many times before.

"You've been avoiding me all night." Rapunzel turned to face him, the layers of her black and gold ballgown feeling excessive by the fire.

"Have I? You know I don't like all of that." He waved his hand toward the din of voices and clink of glasses and scrunched his face in what Rapunzel recognized as disgust.

"I take it that means you've not accepting Leander's offer?"

"I already told him. I want nothing to do with this life…and…" he paused, pinching the bridge of his nose. A few of his locs escaped the neat ponytail he had put them in for this event. "I can't for the life of me understand why you do?"

Rapunzel stared at the flames, its sparks dancing with carefree abandon. The plume of smoke reaching out to the sky. In that moment she wished she could be more carefree like Artemus, but she was scared. Scared to step out of her comfort zone, scared to challenge herself. Instead, she would do what her mother did, take a responsibility that felt like obligation and live and die in Avalonia.

"It's all I have left."

"It's not, but you refuse to see it any other way." He walked away from the fire and back into the thinning crowd. She lost sight of him but hoped that tomorrow cooler heads would prevail, and he would understand why she was choosing to stay.

The celebration lasted long into the night, the music and laughter echoing through the halls as Rapunzel made her way to her new room. It was more opulent than anything Rapunzel had ever lived in. The bed was soft and plush, the drapes made of velvet, furniture hand-carved with tiny flowers. Artemus was shown similar living quarters, but being he chose not to take Leander's offer, she doubted it impressed him.

She stood in front of the mirror and pulled out the pins securing her hair braids in an elaborate updo. It tumbled loose, cascading down her back and over the plush rug. She wasn't ready to cut away all this excess hair, she wanted to hang on to it, and in that way to her mother, for as long as she could.

An envelope propped against the silver candlestick caught her eye. *Zel* written in a familiar scrawl. Artemus. Her heart quickened as she slid a finger under the unsealed flap. Inside was a map and a letter. She unfolded it, the jagged handwriting as wild as the man himself.

Rapunzel,

The open road calls me once more. I cannot ignore the wanderlust pulsing through my veins, urging me to embark on new adventures far from Avalonia. I wish you would come with me, but I won't force your hand.

Though I will miss our exploits, I must forge my own path now, like my father did for himself, and his father before him. You have found your heart's true home, and I wish you joy and prosperity.

If you grow weary of the courtly life, follow the map to the Nordhaven Sea.

Farewell,

Artemus

A hollow ache bloomed in her chest, fingers trembling over the words, tears landing on the words, smudging the farewell. Years together, and it came down to a letter? It slipped from her grasp, falling to the floor. How could he do this to her? She knew he said he would leave, but didn't that warrant a goodbye in person.

She paced the length of the room, suddenly it felt like a prison. A soft knock interrupted her brooding. "Come in."

Leander entered. "I just wanted to check on you. I know there was a lot of people wanting to speak to you. The royal life suits you," he smiled. He noticed her red eyes and the pout on her lips. "What's wrong, Zellie?"

She picked up the letter and handed it to Leander to read, not wanting to read the words herself again. His brow furrowed as he read in silence, he handed it back to her when he finished.

"I take it he didn't let you now he was leaving?"

She shook her head, a fresh wave of tears overwhelming her. Leander wrapped his arms around her and let her cry into his shoulder. He gently rubbed her back, his hands tangled in her hair. She looked up at him, sadness etched in the lines of her face. "How do I go on without him?" Another sob wracked her body.

"Why do you think you need to?" Leander asked, holding her at arm's length so he could stare at her. "It seems to me, you know what you want."

"I want to stay here, where I can continue my mother's work. Where I can be close to her!" She paced the floor again. "Why can't he understand that?"

He grabbed her arm gently and pulled her closer to him. "Zellie, no matter what your hair looks like, how strong your magic is, or where you are in the world; your mother will be close to you." He rubbed her shoulders, her face softened and her lip quivered. "You'll never forget her, no matter how much time passes."

She looked up into Leander's eyes, threw her arms around him. She found comfort in his arms, not the way Artemus made her feel loved and protected, but the comfort of a long-time friend. She knew in that moment that her future wasn't here in Avalonia but wherever she and Artemus were together.

Some time later...

The small hamlet of Haelstrandt was located on the banks of the Nordhaven Sea. Its sole business was a small inn, where fisherman on their way to the would stop to rest. It was one room, barely bigger than someone's sitting room but it was welcoming. Fishing regalia lined the walls, the smell of the sea embedded into the atmosphere.

Rapunzel walked in and sat at the first table near the door. She removed her cape, her shoulder-length hair in one thick braid down her back, the golden strand a little thicker than it had been a few weeks ago. Alderwick taught her a few things before she left; her power was growing everyday.

"Then what happened?" The young girl's voice drifted towards Rapunzel.

"She wrapped her hair around their necks…" Rapunzel paused. She briefly remembered telling Eli that same story before she left. She turned around and saw Artemus sitting by the fire. His smile reaching the corners of his eyes as he tells the girl at his feet the story of the three-headed sea serpent. "When they were stuck together, I took the sword and sliced their heads off in one swing." He stood up, his back tensing up as he pretended to lift a sword high into the air and sliced the air.

"Are you sure it was one swing?" Rapunzel walked towards Artemus, his eyes widened as she came closer.

"Zel, you came?" His hands extended towards her but he was frozen in place.

"Of course I did. When I read your letter, the thought of never seeing you again. I couldn't…" She bit her lip, the time for tears had passed. She melted into his arms, her body knowing how to move and bend until they fit together perfectly.

"Are you sure? You're ready to leave Oakwood and Avalonia?" Their eyes met in an intense moment of knowing. There was no turning back now for either of them.

"I'm ready to live my life, side by side with you." She closed the gap between them, the magic of their kiss filling her up with a sense of belonging she never felt anywhere else.

Also by Vic Leigh, Kristin Boshears, Maria Marandola, and Tammy Godfrey,

Anthologies by Warrioress Publishing.

Desolation of the Sea - A Sapphire City Shared World Dark Fairytale Remake
This may be the darkest reimagining of the Little Mermaid yet. Dive deep into Atlantis located on the outskirts of Sapphire City, and discover a tale of Stockholm syndrome, betrayal, mistrust, and lust. Learn the dark secrets of the Undersea city that will have you reeling with emotion. Are you ready?